Looks can be deceiving.

Herbert leaned forward. "You know what we were talking about last night? How you ought to do something that would really get Superjock's attention?"

I was interested despite myself. "So?"

"So I've been thinking. Brock's used to having women fall for him, right? What really gets to a guy like that is one who doesn't. His interest," Herbert said grandly, "is piqued."

I snorted. "Just assuming I was mad enough to go for this scheme of yours, how am I supposed to put it into practice? In our school, Brock doesn't *have* any competition. If he did, what makes you think I'd have any luck there, either?"

"That's the beauty of this," Herbert said happily. "I mean you and I start going together. For public consumption. That way, everybody will be sure we're both popular, and you can make Superjock jealous. Elegant, isn't it?"

There was a long silence.

"I'm speechless," I said, when I could talk.

"Then you'll do it?"

"No way!"

THE
IMAGE
GAME

NORMA
JOHNSTON

WESTWIND®
Troll

Copyright © 1994 by Dryden Harris St. John, Inc.

Published by WestWind, an imprint and trademark of Troll Communications L.L.C.

First published in hardcover by BridgeWater Books.

Printed in the United States of America.

10 9 8 7 6 5 4 3 2 1

Library of Congress Cataloging-in-Publication Data
Johnston, Norma.
The image game / by Norma Johnston.
p.   cm.
Summary: In an effort to attract high school heartthrob Brock
Peters, Celia changes her outer image.
ISBN 0-8167-3472-0 (lib. bdg.)   ISBN 0-8167-3473-9 (pbk.)
[1. Self-perception—Fiction.   2. High schools—Fiction.
3. Schools—Fiction.]   I. Title.
PZ7.J6453Im   1995
[Fic]—dc20   93-39764

For Joanne Gise Mattern,
who appreciates the real
Susie and Missy,
and understands image games

ONE

The sun was shining, the grass was green, and I was holding forth to Michiko Kimura, with an equal mixture of nobility and altruism, on just why I was going to attend my parents' barbecue that evening instead of keeping our weekly Wednesday night tennis date. Michiko put up with it for five minutes. Then she gave me a look out of those black eyes of hers.

"Come off it, Celia. This is me, remember? The reason you're helping at the barbecue, which ordinarily wild horses couldn't get you near, is because your mother invited all the neighbors, which means Brock Peters will be there."

I turned red. Michiko is my best friend, closer than a sister, and she knows me far too well. "Lenore Collins was Mother's college roommate, and they haven't seen each other for six years. Now that the Collinses have moved to Oakdale, Mom wants to help her and her son get in circulation. If I'm helping because I'm interested in boys, Herbert Collins is the boy, not Brock Peters. And I'm only being a . . . a good neighbor. So don't go telling me there's anything wrong about it."

"I didn't say there was anything wrong about it," Michiko said mildly. "Just that you might as well be honest with me. And with yourself. You're not 'interested in boys,' you're interested in Brock Peters. You have been ever since we were in sixth grade and he was in eighth, and what's wrong with that? Every other girl in school is, too."

"You aren't."

"Oh. Well, I don't have time for that stuff," Michiko said without rancor. I knew what she meant. Michiko's a violinist, a real one, meaning five hours of practice a day and All-State Orchestra as well as the Oakdale Pops, and eventually attending

8

Juilliard. I also knew that as soon as Michiko decides to make time for males, she's going to attract them like honey attracts bears. I'm not, at least not judging from experience.

"Everything's wrong with it." I reverted back to Michiko's question, depression settling like a fog. "Brock doesn't know I'm alive."

"Come *on!* He lives five houses away. He knows you from last year's class elections, and the *Oakleaf,* and goodness knows how many projects at school and church and at the Y."

"Oh, sure. Brock knows me as the kid who did his paper route for him when he had junior high football practice, and who makes posters and works on committees. Good old dependable Celia. He never sees me as a *girl.* He's too busy looking Laurie Malone up and down!"

"I'm glad he *doesn't* know you in some of the ways he probably knows Laurie," Michiko said primly. Then she laughed. "That was mean. Laurie's nice."

"Also gorgeous. Also a senior, head cheerleader, shoo-in for next June's Citizenship Award for girls, and—what do you call it? Charismatic."

Michiko stopped in the middle of Prospect Street, turned me around, and shook me. "Celia, stop it. There's nothing wrong with you, and a lot that's right. And if Brock hasn't woken up to that, then it's his loss."

"There's a lot wrong, next to Laurie. I'm too—plain vanilla. I don't stand out in a crowd."

"With that red hair?" Michiko scoffed.

"Next to the hair the rest of me is colorless. And my hair's not red. Dark red would be dramatic. It's orange."

"Your dad doesn't do so bad with it," Michiko murmured dryly. I chuckled. Dad's lawyer/manager of our area's public TV station, and a smash hit as emcee of its annual telethon. He's acquired a bunch of groupies and the nickname Eric the Red, on account of his blazing beard.

"Anyway," Michiko went on encouragingly, "you have a great sense of humor, when you let it show."

"You mean a weird one. Also like Dad."

"And you're going to be features editor of the *Oakleaf* this coming year. That makes you noticeable. And proves you're popular."

"It proves Ms. Blauvelt knows I'm

dependable. You know darn well the faculty adviser picks the school newspaper staff."

"And she picked Laurie Malone as editor in chief." Michiko had a glint in her eye. "So what does that prove?"

"It proves I'll be right in the middle of the magic circle," I admitted, "which is the point you're trying to make." I laughed, starting to feel better. "Like you said, you know me, so why waste the effort being subtle?"

Michiko just smiled and gave me a push. "Go on home and wash your hair. It's full of chlorine from the pool. And wear your blue Indian dress—it looks great on you."

"Want to come to the barbecue?"

"You don't need me there for moral support," Michiko said dryly. "You'll be one girl to two guys. Make the most of it." She was right; there were no other teenagers among the families my parents had invited. "Anyway, I got Roberta Wills to fill in for you, so I'll still play tennis. Mom has ten fits when I miss a game. She thinks I don't get enough fresh air and exercise."

I groaned. "Where have I heard that before?"

"You're not a bit sorry to miss the game," Michiko pointed out all too accurately. "You like exercise about as much as a Persian cat does."

"And you like Dad's barbecues just about as much."

Michiko grinned. "I hope your mother's doing some of the cooking, too."

"She is. And she has some fried chicken being sent in, just in case." We reached Michiko's corner and I said, "Come over in the morning, as soon as you finish practicing."

"Call me after everybody goes home tonight, if you can. I want to hear what happens!" Michiko darted off, a bright bird in her turquoise top and fuchsia shorts, and I went home to be handmaiden to my father's culinary endeavors.

Three years ago Mother and I gave Dad a deluxe gas barbecue outfit for his birthday, and it was a big mistake. His enthusiasm for it is as great as his skill is not. By now the neighbors had gotten used to underdone chicken and charred ribs, but it was a pity to inflict them on the Collinses.

It was a pity to inflict them on Brock.

Brock. Brock Peters. Senior, letterman, undoubtedly upcoming president of the Student Council. Brock, with his thick, light brown hair, silvered now by the sun; his olive skin that had a year-round tan; his green eyes that had magic in them when he smiled. Brock moved to town four summers ago, when he was about to go into eighth grade and I into sixth, and I fell head over heels. I'm still fallen.

Enough of that, I told myself sternly. It was the new kid, Herbert Collins, I was supposed to be concerned about, and a fine welcomer to the neighborhood I'd be if my mind was all on Brock. I hurried the remaining six blocks to the Elephant, which is what we call our house. As in white elephant. It started out around the turn of the century as one of those brown-shingled crosses between a cottage and a barn. A generation or two later some misguided soul painted it white and added porches and southern mansion columns. It has a thirty-foot living room, tons of bedrooms, and too few baths, and Mother's always saying what a wonderful place it is for growing up and having parties.

Today I found my mother calmly moving around the porch, putting flowers on the tables while my father whistled happily amid a cloud of smoke in the side yard. Mother looked up with relief as I clattered up the steps, pushing off an onrush of German shepherd and Shetland sheepdog.

"Susabelle! Melissa! Let Celia alone! You'd think you hadn't seen her for a month instead of just four hours. Cele, you'd better hurry up and change. I was getting worried."

"I meant to get back sooner," I said. "How're things going?"

"Fine, except that Susie stole one of your father's racks of spareribs. I don't think she was impressed by them," Mother said judiciously. "She left them in the middle of the living-room floor. Dare I suggest it's a pity she didn't go back for more?"

I grinned. Dad believes that where garlic and red pepper are concerned, if a little's good, a lot is that much better. "I won't quote you. But I also won't help you frame Susie; Dad's still mad at her for eating up his income tax form last spring. Any word from the Collinses?"

"They've arrived!" Mother positively sparkled. "The moving men are still there, but their phone's installed, and Lenore promises they'll be here by six. I can't *wait* to see her." She anxiously smoothed her aqua slacks. "Do I look all right? Do you think I've put on weight?"

"You? You never put on weight. You look exactly like your college pictures. I wonder if Aunt Lenore's as well preserved." She was my godmother, and I'd been taught to think of her as Aunt Lenore, even though I hadn't seen her since before my brother Joey, now eight, was born. I had only the vaguest recollection of her son. Herbert—what a name!

"Don't you get smart-mouthed! Well preserved, indeed—Lenore's only forty-two, the same as me. And she probably looks younger." Mother looked at her watch and jumped. "You'd better get dressed. And see if you can find out what your brother's up to. He's *supposed* to be dressing."

I went into the house, trailing my canine ladies-in-waiting, and encountered my brother sliding down the banister. The best way I can describe Joey is to say he's the kind of kid who sleeps in his soccer cap and still has the first dimes he conned out of younger kids via a "Ten Cents to See the Monster" (a dead lizard) show in our garage. He has Mother's dark hair and dark eyes, and a smile that can melt an iceberg.

In short, he's definitely going to be another Brock Peters in a few years.

At this moment, like most moments, he was very grungy. I caught him as he tumbled off the newel post and turned him firmly toward the stairs. "Go take a shower! At once!" Then I thought better of it. "No! *I* get the bathroom first." Joey uses up a whole day's supply of hot water in a single shower. "You go to your room and stay there. It might not be a bad idea to do some picking up; Mom's probably going to want to show Aunt Lenore the house. The bathroom will be yours in ten minutes, understand?"

"My room's always picked up," Joey said with dignity. That wasn't a lie, merely his misguided opinion. As in: Smelly sneakers belong in the middle of the floor, and why make a bed if you're only going to have to unmake it to get back in? Not to mention discarded snakeskins and worse (not all of it deceased) as room decor. I shuddered, went to my own room to contemplate my image in the mirror, and shuddered again.

Michiko might think I was *noticeable* in a positive sense, but Michiko was kind. The mirror showed, all too clearly, that I'd gotten into the habit of raiding the icebox since school let out. And I'd been in the sun too long today, which meant that where my fair skin wasn't peeling, it was turning red. My hair was like rusty straw.

And Brock would be here. Aunt Lenore's son, too, of course, but he didn't count. I had a sudden image of Laurie Malone's Homecoming Queen perfection, and bolted for the bathroom where steam would mercifully blur the mirror's truth.

I was out only five minutes later than my optimistic estimate, hair streaming like wet seaweed but at least clean. I collared Joey, gave him firm instructions about scrubbing himself everywhere and hanging up towels when he was through, and returned to my room to do the best I could with the materials at hand. Hair back? I tried it and considered. Better than frizzing or hanging down wet, I decided, shoving in combs. Then the crinkled-cotton dress from India, a vibrant turquoise blue. Bright blue was supposed to be good for redheads. Now the eye shadow that I'd bought to match.

I still didn't look as good as Laurie Malone. Or Michiko. Or, for that matter, my mother. Oh, the hell with it, I thought savagely, jamming my feet into sandals and

17

running downstairs just as the doorbell started ringing.

Our front door's one of those Dutch ones; the top and bottom can open separately. Right now the bottom half was closed to keep the dogs inside, and through the open top I saw a vibrant woman who reminded me, all too much, of Laurie. I mean *perfection*; blond hair simply and artfully cut in a geometric shape; blue-green eyes; a no-makeup look that every woman knows means a lot of art and cash. And, when she saw me, a wide, delighted smile.

"Celia! I can't get over how you've grown! Oh, I'm sorry; that was stupid and you must hate hearing it." Aunt Lenore hugged me over the top of the closed half-door. "The last time I saw you, you were a skinny seven-year-old. Oh, it's so *good* to be here!" she exclaimed, as Mother came running up the porch steps to hug her from behind.

All the excitement brought the dogs, barking like crazy, and then Joey, rakishly wrapped in a towel. Mother sent "the girls," as she calls the dogs, and my brother upstairs, and we settled on the wicker furniture on the side porch. My father detached himself from the barbecue—more hugs, more exclamations. Mother looked around and pulled herself up. "Lenore! Where's Herbie?"

Aunt Lenore grimaced. "Marge, I'm sorry. He just wouldn't come, and he disappeared before I could apply physical force. You have no idea how that child hates social affairs. Especially intergenerational ones with a lot of people he doesn't know."

Mother looked disappointed, but my heart sang within me. No Herbie—no new-kid-in-the-neighborhood duties falling on my shoulders. I could focus my hostessing attentions on Brock. I blushed, and hoped nobody saw.

Dad looked amused. "Sounds like the boy shows good taste and discrimination, considering some of the intergenerational shindigs I've been dragged to."

"Now, Eric, don't you take his part! I'm hoping you Prendergasts can knock some sense into him!" Aunt Lenore shook her head. "I worry about him. These past four years since his father died, he must have missed having a man around, and I've had to be so wrapped up in my work. Retailing's just not a nine-to-five, forty-hour-a-week job, particularly if you're in management . . . I'm not sure what age level

Herbie's at, ten years or fifty, but he sure isn't like any seventeen-year-old I've ever known! He's not the least interested in a social life."

"What is he interested in?" Dad asked.

"I couldn't begin to explain," Aunt Lenore answered wryly. "I'm not math- and science-minded. He'll probably tell *you*. He can hold forth for hours on subjects that excite him, but not to people his own age. He thinks it's a waste of time."

"As I said, a man of taste and discernment," Dad murmured. There was a secret-joke tone in his voice that made me prick up my ears. I looked up, and saw my father gazing not at me but clear across the porch, across the lawn, to where three figures were approaching. Mr. and Mrs. Peters. And Brock.

I was immediately, to my great disgust, confused and tongue-tied. Blessedly, Brock was not. Brock was striding forward, his hand out. "Mr. Prendergast. Nice to see you, sir. Mrs. Prendergast, thank you for asking me. Hello, Celia!"

He was holding my right hand in both of his and smiling that crooked smile, with his eyes crinkled, that seemed to create an intimate little island for the two of us. "What have you been doing since school let out? Coming up with any ideas for overhauling the *Oakleaf*'s feature pages?"

He remembered I was going to be the features editor . . . "Something like that," I murmured breathlessly.

"Great! I have some ideas for it, too. I'd like to get the paper really involved in local issues, not just school stuff. I hope you'll give me a chance to get together with you about it later. Kick it around, just the two of us?"

"I'd like that."

"Great! It's a date, then," Brock smiled again and gave my hand a little squeeze. Then he turned to be introduced to Aunt Lenore, the very model of a high school leader. I could hear the wishful thinking going on in Aunt Lenore's head.

"I'm sorry my son isn't here to meet you."

Brock laughed. "That's okay. You know how guys are—throw us down in a strange place and two hours later we've found our own things to do and places we want to go!" He was throwing a mantle of eligible bachelorhood over Herbert, and I blessed him for it as Aunt Lenore's face eased. "We'll bump into each other at the pool, or somewhere. I'll be glad to take him around, show him the ropes."

"That would be marvelous. I'll tell him." Aunt Lenore smiled, but I could tell she was none too hopeful. Then everybody else in the neighborhood began arriving, and I was swallowed up in the normal chaos of a Prendergast party.

Mom and Dad had been extravagant, as usual, with invitations. Little kids barreled about, with Joey in the lead. The dogs, imprisoned on the third floor, keened as though they were mourners at a wake till Joey, strictly against orders, let them loose. Then they came on like cyclones, scaring the wits out of old Mr. and Mrs. McKenna, who live next door and ought to be used to it by now, and alternately stealing food and begging for it like perfect ladies. What with coping with all this, and running back and forth from the kitchen with serving dishes, I didn't get a chance to look for Brock again till everyone was settled down on the porch and lawn in small groups, eating.

I couldn't find him.

What I did find was Susie, who had found my purse and dragged it outside to investigate beneath the lilac bushes. I rescued it, looped it over my shoulder, and locked Susie in the laundry room to meditate on her sins. Then, while inside, I checked the kitchen, the living and dining rooms, Dad's study. No Brock Peters.

He wasn't on the side porch with his parents, or on the steps. Finally, carrying a plate of hot rolls as my excuse, I approached my father, who was putting his gas grill to bed. "Have you seen Brock? I thought he might like another roll."

Dad's face was inscrutable. "He left. He asked me if we'd mind, since Herbert Collins hadn't come and there was none of the school crowd here. I told him we'd survive."

None of the school crowd here. He hadn't been interested in talking with me. He was only being polite. He didn't even think of me—if he thought of me at all—as a part of Oakdale High.

My eyes stung, and my hand started to shake. I set the plate of rolls down on the shelf of Dad's beloved grill. "Give these to Mom for me, will you?" I mumbled. "I guess I'm . . . not really needed here any longer, either."

And I cut out.

TWO

I didn't know where I was going. I didn't much care, so long as it wasn't past Brock's house or any of the places he might hang around. Or past the tennis court. I didn't want to face Michiko's sympathy till I'd concocted a very funny story to explain the defection of both Herbert Collins and Brock Peters.

My feet led me up the road behind our street, past the land that was once a farm and pond and was now older-adults-only condominiums, and back into the rolling hills. I hadn't come walking up here for a long time—not since I'd started high school, probably. This was old-time Oakdale, and I'd forgotten how beautiful it could be. There weren't any high-priced housing developments here yet, only low, eighteenth-century New Jersey Dutch stone houses and comfortably shabby Victorian wooden ones, and here and there a new one, expensive but set back so it blended in.

I leaned my arms on somebody's fence rail and took a deep breath. The air smelled of swamp and skunk cabbage, all overlaid with wild roses and honeysuckle. It smelled of childhood.

I shook my head and pulled myself back on track. I should be able to get home before dark if I cut through Dynachem's private drive. Dynachem Industries, which started out as a chemical firm in its founder's garage and is now a multinational conglomerate, built its regional headquarters in Oakdale right before we moved here. Thanks to local planning board requirements, you can't quite tell whether the place is a factory, a palace, or a park. Part of the grounds are open to the public, and you can catch New Jersey's famous catfish in its streams.

The entrance was tastefully adorned with

rhododendron bushes, sheets of purple and white petunias, and loads of traffic lights. There wasn't any traffic now. I plodded along the curving drive past the company tennis court, wishing I'd had the foresight to change my sandals for tennis shoes. Low to my left, the stream beckoned. The banks were occupied by sleepy Canada geese, but they were as tame as could be. I started across the grass, picking my way among the gray-brown forms.

I was almost to the water's edge before it dawned on me that one of the forms was not a goose. It wasn't even feathered. It was sticking up in the air and was undoubtedly a human rump. A male rump, judging from the size of the feet belonging to it.

I turned and was making silently for the drive again when a voice hailed me. "Hey, you! You wouldn't have a plastic bag with you, would you?"

Mother would not have approved. I answered before I thought. "A *what?*"

"A plastic bag. For the turtle," the voice said reasonably. The shape turned itself around and unfolded into something identifiable. Sex: male. Age: about the same as mine. Size: very tall. Hair: blond; needed cutting. Appearance: strange. I don't mean strange in the sense that would make Mother hiss, "Celia, get out of there!" On the contrary, she'd probably think him cute! Me, I don't find a six-foot-two male in a mechanic's jumpsuit with the sleeves cut off, and thick glasses, particularly endearing. But he did look harmless.

"What's with the turtle?" I asked warily. I shot a glance around. Somebody was mowing the grass across the drive, and two men were fishing farther up the stream, so if this guy turned out to be a weirdo, I'd have rescuers. Besides, by now Scarecrow in the jumpsuit was holding a large brown object out toward me beseechingly.

It really was a turtle. Its head thrust out, swinging from side to side, and its legs thrashed aimlessly. "I thought turtles pulled in to avoid strangers," I said as I stepped closer.

"They do. This guy knows he's in trouble, and he knows I'm a friend. Grab hold of him, will you? I don't want to try to climb out of this muck with him for fear I'll skid and drop him. Don't you step in the mud."

He leaned as far forward as he could, holding the turtle out at arm's length. And so help me, I took it. In my blue gauze dress and all. The turtle and I eyed each other gingerly.

"He won't bite. Just get a firm grip on the outer edges of his shell so he can't wriggle free, and be careful of the center section of the shell. It's cracked." He scrambled up as I held the turtle carefully. Fortunately, the turtle was acting resigned. "What about the plastic bag?"

"Sorry, I didn't come out prepared for a reptile hunt. What do you want it for, anyway?"

"To put this guy in so I can carry him home. My mother's not going to be too thrilled if I bring him in dripping muck all over her new pale blue carpet." He looked me up and down critically. "I don't suppose you're wearing anything you could tear a piece of material off of, are you?"

"No way! I do have a pair of scissors in my bag, in case *you're* wearing anything you can spare," I added pointedly.

"These are my favorite work clothes. Oh, well. I'll take the turtle back, and you hack the legs off around cutoff level, will you? Then we can make 'em into a kind of bag for our friend here."

So instead of scoring points with Brock, there I was, as a beautiful sunset spread across the sky, on my knees on Dynachem's rolling lawn, cutting the pant legs off a boy I'd never seen before. "Hurry up," he said anxiously as I sawed through the heavy denim. "Theodore here's starting to get restless."

"How do you know it's a he? No, don't tell me! What are you going to do with him?" I looked at the cracked shell thoughtfully. "You could take him to the wildlife center in the morning."

"The wildlife center sounds like a good idea. But first I'm going to take him home and mend his shell with epoxy. It'll work. I've done it a couple of times before, on other turtles." He turned the turtle expertly, examining it, as I watched him with new respect.

"Scientist?"

"Getting there. I was concentrating on chemistry, but now I'm really getting into marine biology. Can't you do that any faster?"

"No, sir. Not really, sir. And if you're out collecting specimens, why didn't you bring some plastic bags of your own along?"

29

"I wasn't expecting to collect specimens," he said mildly. "I just happened to be checking out the area when I spotted Theodore having trouble. I think some kids must have thrown rocks at him." He stroked the turtle's head with a gentle finger. "Look at that face. Doesn't he look like an old Buddha?"

"He looks like he's awfully lucky you came along." I finished cutting through the second pant leg. "Okay, step out."

"If you cut strips from one piece, you can tie—"

"I can make a bag. I know! But there's no reason I have to do it here in the wet. There's no reason I have to do it at all, if you come down to it." I picked up the tubes of denim as he kicked free of them, and headed firmly up the bank. He followed, chastened.

"I'm sorry. I didn't mean to start a war." He plopped down full length on the grass beside me, placing Theodore carefully on his stomach. "It's extremely magnanimous and humanitarian of you to interrupt your— what were you doing here, anyway? Jogging?"

"I'm not much into jogging."

"Anyway, Theodore and I are very grateful. Say thank you, Theodore." The turtle ignored us. "Sorry, he's not much into speaking."

"You're an idiot," I said sternly.

"So I've been told. Particularly by my mother. For some unfathomable reason, she's concluded she's failing as a parent if she doesn't turn me into Best All-Around, Best Liked, etcetera, etcetera, etcetera." He stroked the turtle's head, and Theodore's eyes took on that glazed look Susie and Missy get when their ears are scratched. "She's afraid that in adolescents a dedication to anything other than chasing the opposite sex is a sign of a maladjusted personality."

I grinned. "I know a lot of parents who would be glad to swap places with her!"

"Yours?"

"No, I—my mom would be inclined to agree with your mother." I meant to say that lightly, jokingly, but suddenly the memory of Brock Peters walking out without a word welled up.

Face it, when I'd been sawing the coverall legs just now, I'd been fantasizing what it would be like if it had been *Brock* there with the turtle, in need of me. *Hadn't* I?

Oh, Mother might think I was socially backward, not interested in dating yet, but she didn't know the half of it!

I turned away abruptly. Behind my

shoulder a male voice said with concern, "Hey, if I hit a raw nerve, I'm sorry."

"It wasn't you. I just realized I'm the one who's an idiot."

"Want to talk about it? I may not be Most Popular, but sometimes verbalizing to a stranger helps. And I am a good listener."

"Purely in the interests of science, of course."

"Of course." He rummaged for a Kleenex and thrust it in my hand. It was pretty grungy, but I wiped my eyes, anyway. My carefully applied eye makeup came off, but that didn't matter, anyway, with Brock not here to see.

"What is it, pressure to go with guys? Or with *a* guy? Or is it a guy who doesn't know you're alive?"

"That was sharp," I said when I could speak.

He shrugged. "Not really. Statistically, males mature later than females, and when immature they usually fall for women who are dim but dazzling. Which you're not."

"Thanks a whole heap."

"Would you want to be dim?" he asked reasonably. "Maybe you'd better finish that bag while you're talking. Theodore's starting to revive."

"There isn't much to talk about. There's

somebody in school I like. Everybody likes. He's that kind."

"Star athlete? President of his class?"

"You got it."

"Everything my mother wishes."

"Don't you?" I asked involuntarily. He shook his head.

"I could care less. Unless I didn't have to give up other things to have it, and there aren't enough hours in the day now for things that are really fun. Get back to Superjock. Why haven't you done things to get his notice?"

"I have! I live down the street from him. I'm in all his clubs. I was his assistant campaign manager." I laughed ruefully. "I did his paper route."

"He probably has lots of women to do those things. You need a different angle. Something that would set you apart." He contemplated his middle. "How about giving him a pet turtle?"

"I don't think Brock would be thrilled. I know his mother wouldn't be." I held out the sack I'd concocted and together we edged Theodore into it. "I'm afraid you're stuck with Theodore," I said, tying a strip of denim firmly around the open end.

"He lives down the street? How about the feed-the-brute, give-him-a-shoulder-to-cry-on routine?"

"Brock's not the crying type. And he's so uninterested in our cuisine he didn't even bother staying for dinner at our house tonight. Not that I blame him," I said laughingly, salvaging my pride. "My father's absolutely awful at the outdoor grill! As a matter of fact, I sneaked away myself. That's the only reason you had my magnificent help in rescuing Theodore!"

"Theodore and I couldn't be happier." He laid the sack carefully on the grass and sat up. "Hey, you haven't eaten, then? Neither have I. Is there a place around here we could go for hamburgers? My treat."

I had a sudden vision of walking into McDonald's, full of people from the tennis courts and softball fields, with this apparition complete with swamp mud and bagged turtle. Fortunately, my face didn't betray my feelings. Or maybe he simply didn't notice. He was going on happily, "This is really interesting. You just happened to come here because you were avoiding a dumb social event, and so did I. Would you believe it, our first night in town and already my mother's trying to fix me up with some dimwit?"

An awful suspicion gripped me.

"What dimwit?" I asked carefully.

"I don't remember the name. But I know she's a dimwit because all the way from Indiana Mom's been babbling about how wonderful it is that her old college roommate has a daughter just the right age, who knows everybody and is into everything in school. And how she'd *love* to 'get me started on the right track socially,' if I'd only 'position myself correctly' and 'maximize my options.'" He grinned. "I think I have the words straight. Mom tends to talk like an M.B.A. textbook since she's been in upper management. Come on, let's take Theodore to get a hamburger."

I stepped back. "The dimwit's name," I said carefully, "is Celia Prendergast. And you have one thing wrong. She doesn't have any interest at all in 'getting you on the right track' in Oakdale. Frankly, Herbert Collins, given your prejudices and peculiarities, it would be a lost cause!"

For the second time that night, I made a speedy exit. I only wished it was a grand one!

THREE

I awoke, too early, the next morning. The phone rang soon thereafter, while I was contemplating the disaster of the night before. At this hour it just had to be Michiko, wanting gory details.

I picked up the receiver and said grumpily, "Couldn't you stand the suspense for another hour?"

"What suspense?" a voice, decidedly not Michiko's, asked blankly. "This is Celia Prendergast, isn't it? Herbert Collins here. It *was* you playing paramedic to a turtle last night, wasn't it?"

"It was," I said.

"That's what I deduced after you stormed off," Herbert said happily. "Look, about your problem—"

I counted to ten and then spoke carefully. "Other than being woken up at six A.M., I wasn't aware I *had* a problem. *You're* the one with Theodore on your hands."

"Is it only six? I didn't notice. Theodore's fine, by the way. I was checking on him just now and I had a brainstorm," Herbert went on with enthusiasm. "About your Brock character. I think you and I can work a deal to our mutual advantage. You want to meet me downtown for breakfast so we can talk about it?"

"You actually want to have breakfast with a dimwit?"

"What dimwit?" Herbert asked blankly. "If you don't want to go out, can I come over there? We don't have any groceries in this place yet."

I considered. I certainly didn't want to go out to eat with Huck Finn in a cutoff jumpsuit, not after that crack he'd made. On the other hand, if I fed him here, I'd win Brownie points with Mother and Aunt Lenore. It would give me great satisfaction to hear what he had in mind and then give him a hard time. It would salve my wounded pride to be able to tell Michiko about it.

"Okay," I said shortly. "But don't show up for half an hour."

At least I didn't have to bother fussing with my looks for Herbert Collins. I pulled on shorts and a T-shirt, went downstairs and took waffles and sausages from the freezer, and said, "All right, already," to Missy and Susie, who by now were going crazy at the door.

We were exploring the peony patch in the far corner of the side lawn when we encountered Herbert, looking exactly the same as when I'd left him the night before, except minus mud. The girls went crazy, of course, and Herbert plopped down on the grass and let them crawl all over him. "Nice animals," he said at last, holding Susie off so she couldn't lick his face. My estimation of him went up a few notches. It wasn't everyone who could withstand that onslaught.

"Come on," I said, relenting, and yanked on their leashes. Herbert followed me back to the house.

"Good thing I didn't bring Theodore along," he murmured.

"Are you kidding? Susie's scared to death of turtles, ever since one nipped her nose when she was a pup. We get a lot of turtles showing up on roads and lawns, now that the open land around here is getting built up."

"Like the Dynachem plant, you mean? Nice-looking place, but industrial parks upset the ecological balance no matter how careful they try to be."

I was about to ask him if ecological balance was what he'd come to discuss, when Joey barreled in, dressed tastefully in underpants and soccer cap. I told him to go get decent. Joey made a rude noise, threw a few more sausages in the microwave, and stared at Herbert.

Herbert bent down and stuck out his hand. "I'm Herbert Collins. Who are you?"

Joey was enchanted, particularly when he heard the tale of Theodore. He was all for going over to be introduced immediately, and when that didn't work he planted himself between us at the kitchen table and monopolized the conversation.

"What did you want to talk to me about?" I asked Herbert at last, loudly.

"Inadvisable to submit sensitive negotiations to scrutiny of minor members of the firm," Herbert said with meaning.

"You don't have to talk over my head," Joey said, injured. He slid off his chair. "I can take a hint."

"Good man. You don't have to leave. Celia and I can go outside, right?" Herbert asked me. I nodded. By now we were beginning to hear my parents' voices, anyway.

We went out on the side porch and settled ourselves in the big wicker chairs. "Now that I've fed you, what do you want?" I asked ungraciously.

Herbert's eyebrows rose. "What are you so sore about? I thought we were getting along fine till you took off like a bat out of hell last night." He leaned forward. "You know what we were talking about? How you ought to do something that would really get Superjock's attention?"

I was interested despite myself. "So?"

"So I've been thinking. Brock's used to having women fall for him, right? What really gets to a guy like that is one who doesn't. His interest," Herbert said grandly, "is piqued."

I snorted. "As Joey would say, *yeeccchhh!* He'd never notice. What's one absentee among all the females swooning at his feet?"

"Ah, but you've missed the whole point. She's *not* invisible. She stands out, because she's fallen madly and passionately for the competition!"

"Your mother's right. You are weird," I said at last. "Just assuming I was mad enough to go for this scheme of yours, how am I supposed to put it into practice? In our school Brock doesn't *have* any competition. If he did, what makes you think I'd have any luck there, either?"

"That's the beauty of this," Herbert said happily. "I told you I was talking about a deal. Remember what I was saying about Ma being on my back because I wasn't concerned enough about being socially adjusted? I'm darned if I'm going to waste time and money trying to win a popularity contest. But as it is, I waste time arguing, and it's getting her upset, which she really doesn't need. So it hit me, when I was patching up Theodore's shell this morning: We both need surrogates!"

"What?"

"Surrogates. Artificial entities, substantively different but indistinguishable from the real thing, and serving the same purpose."

"As Joey said, you don't have to talk over my head. I'm not a scientist."

"Sorry. I mean you and I start going together. For public consumption, I mean. That way, everybody will be sure we're both popular, you can make Superjock jealous, and Ma will breathe a sigh of relief and get off my case. Elegant, isn't it?" Herbert sat back, beaming like a puppy waiting to be patted.

There was a long silence.

"I'm speechless," I said, when I could talk.

"Then you'll do it?"

"No way!"

"Why not?" Herbert demanded, injured.

"Because," I said brutally, "the last thing that would make Brock jealous is my being seen dating a nerd. It would just confirm his convictions I'm not romance material. If he has any convictions about me at all, that is. The last thing *I* want is to spend time with a weirdo, too."

Herbert blinked behind his glasses. "Am I really that objectionable?"

He looked like a puppy again. A hurt one. I remembered his concern and efficiency with the turtle, his sympathy about my plight with Brock, and I melted.

"No, you're not," I answered honestly. "But

it's the way you look—the way you act—do you have to make me spell it out? High school seniors who are Most Likely to Succeed do not go around wearing weird-looking sleeveless jumpsuits with holes in them in embarrassing places! They don't avoid parties given in their honor. They don't pick up girls by asking them to join them in the mud. Or by offering them a—what did you call it? A mutually advantageous deal!"

"It piqued your interest, didn't it?"

"And they're not called Herbert!"

"That's my name," Herbert pointed out. But he looked deflated.

"Anyway," I went on, reddening, "I shouldn't think you'd want to be seen with a dimwit, either."

Herbert scratched his head. "You seem to have some kind of fixation on this dimwit business. Would you mind explaining?"

"Don't you remember? You couldn't be bothered coming here last night because, and I quote, you didn't want to have this dimwitted female thrown at you."

Illumination dawned. "But I didn't *know* you then," Herbert pointed out reasonably. "I've seen the girls Ma's tried to get me interested in before. I've heard her babbling

43

all my life about the grand old times she and your mother had at college, and the traps they laid for guys, and the wild weekends, and all the rest. I used to hear her on the phone to your mother when I was a kid, rattling on about how great it would be if you and I hit it off when we grew up. I even saw pictures of your dance recitals, and of the Little Miss beauty contest you won at the Jersey shore. How could I expect you to be anything but a dimwit?"

I was totaling up a list of subjects about which Mother and I were going to have a serious talk.

"Anyway," Herbert finished, "you're not a dimwit. You're *sensible*." To him, that was clearly the highest compliment. "So how about it?" Then his face fell. "Oh, I forgot. You don't want to be seen dating a nerd."

I sat there and looked at him. And I thought. I could feel a smile starting to spread across my face.

"There would have to be some changes made," I said slowly.

"What kind of changes?" Herbert did a double take. "You mean you'll do it?"

"Maybe. You said this was a business proposition. We have to talk terms."

Herbert draped his legs over the arm of his chair and got comfortable. "Okay, shoot."

"You have to let me make you over. On the outside, that is," I added hastily as he frowned. "You're into earth sciences. You know even diamonds need cutting and polishing. So does your hair! And clothes. And social graces."

"I'm not spending money on a lot of rags I can't stand," Herbert said firmly.

"Agreed. You have to think they're at least bearable."

"And I don't want to waste a lot of time doing things that aren't bearable, either." He looked resigned. "I suppose we'll have to go to some dances, won't we? I have two left feet."

"I'll teach you. And sports. You have to go out for sports."

"I draw the line at ball playing." Herbert set his chin. It wasn't a bad chin, I noticed irrelevantly. "A bunch of grown men chasing a ball around a field or court is one of the silliest things I know. I wouldn't mind racquetball; that's good for coordination. We could have some racquetball or tennis dates, couldn't we? That would kill two birds with one ball." He looked pleased at the joke. "Or we could go bike riding. There are some real good nature trails within twenty miles of here, I hear."

I winced. "I hate a lot of physical activities myself."

"They'll do you good." Herbert looked me over critically. "You could stand to lose ten pounds. Fair's fair. If you can't afford to be seen with a dog, I can't, either."

I winced again. "Okay." I looked him squarely in the eye. "Each of us has the right to request changes of the other, provided we can back up the request with good reasons. Each of us has the right to refuse requests that really . . ." I fished for words.

"That really violate our personal integrity," Herbert said solemnly. His eyes twinkled.

I grinned back. "You got it. And we're going to be seen together enough to—to achieve our objectives, but we're not going to monopolize each other's private life. And if either of us gets an invitation from somebody else that's absolutely irresistible—"

"We negotiate," Herbert said. "Okay, then. Does that mean we're going together?"

"I guess we are," I said weakly.

Herbert stood up, all six feet two inches of him. I stood up, too. We shook hands solemnly. "It's a deal."

FOUR

For a minute we just stood there awkwardly. Then the telephone began to ring, and I took a deep breath and started to laugh. "That'll be Michiko. I can't wait to tell her what we've cooked up!"

Herbert grabbed my arm. "Wait a minute! We don't tell anybody! That's part of the deal."

"I don't intend to tell 'anybody,'" I said with dignity. "Michiko's my best friend. She's also an absolute clam."

"She could be deaf and blind and I wouldn't feel any better," Herbert said. "I don't want any of this leaking back to my mother. It would defeat the whole purpose. Besides, do you really want to take a chance of anything getting back to your Prince Charming?"

No, I didn't. More to the point, I didn't want anything reaching Joey, who has a broadcast range equal to Dad's TV station. Herbert was right. We mustn't tell a soul.

"Celia! Telephone!" came Mother's voice from the kitchen. I gave Herbert a push. "Go home before she sees you!"

"Don't you think I should introduce myself?"

I looked at him, then down at myself. Neither of us looked that good. I shook my head.

Herbert's eyes crinkled. All at once we were both thinking of the same thing—last night's mud and muck and Theodore. "I'll go home and clean up," Herbert said solemnly. "If Ma hasn't left for work, I'll mumble something about bumping into you last night and how you weren't as bad as I expected, helping with Theodore and all. I guess I'd better break the news about Theodore to her, too. He and I were both asleep when she came home last night. I'll bring Theodore over to call on you this afternoon. Is around three okay? Are sneakers acceptable, or should I put on shoes? Shall I bring you flowers, or would that be overdoing it?"

Thank goodness he had a sense of humor. Maybe this wasn't going to be as bad as I'd expected.

"Sneakers are fine, but skip the jumpsuit, can you? Try a shirt and jeans. The flowers," I said demurely, "are up to you."

"*Celia!*" Mother repeated.

Herbert, so help me, bowed from the waist. "'Parting is such sweet sorrow—'"

"Will you get out of here? Good-bye, Herbert—" I stopped. "Doesn't *anybody* call you anything else? That name makes me think of somebody's straightlaced stuffed-shirt uncle."

"Grandfather," Herbert corrected. "And he wasn't stuffy. I can't help it if I was named for both my grandfathers. Herbert Zachary Collins." He grimaced. "Ma, would you believe it, still calls me *Herbie* sometimes. But I'd belt anybody else who tried it."

"*Wait a minute.* Zachary. *Zack.*" I considered. "It's good. No, actually, it's great."

"Okay, Zack it is." He gave me a friendly salute and took off.

Just in time. Mother came out, inquiring tartly whether I was deaf or moonstruck. "Michiko's on the phone. She wants to know how meeting Herbert Collins went. Too bad you don't have anything to tell her," Mother finished ruefully.

"Oh, yes, I have some stuff to tell you about that," I murmured vaguely, and went inside to practice my spiel on Michiko first.

It seemed advisable to stay pretty true to facts about last night, so I did, except for being vague about Herbert's personal appearance. I even included the bit about his assuming Celia Prendergast was a dimwit, and how I'd flounced off, since it was pretty funny, all things considered.

Michiko was properly sympathetic. "What was he like?"

"Scientific. Enthusiastic about marine biology. And turtles."

"You *are* a dimwit. What does he look like, you idiot?"

"Tall."

"As tall as Brock?"

"A lot taller. Blond hair. Blue eyes."

There was a pause. I could almost hear the wheels going around in Michiko's head. "Hmmmm," she said at last. "Maybe he would do to make Brock jealous."

"Maybe I wouldn't mind." That was enough of a first seed to plant. "Talk to you later. I have to go help clear out the rest of last night's mess."

"I wish I could clear Brock Peters out," Michiko said. "Preferably in little pieces. He and Laurie showed up at Christensen's last night after he left your place, in case you're interested." Christensen's is our local ice-cream parlor.

"Thanks a whole heap," I said tartly, and went to feed my mother an account of Romeo and Juliet meeting romantically by the Dynachem stream.

"At least he was out enjoying himself," Mother said, starting to laugh. "Poor Lenore! She's always been totally unflappable, but she's getting herself into a real stew worrying whether Herbie's having a satisfactorily happy adolescence!"

I snorted. "Since when is adolescence sweetness and light and fun and games!"

"Only in retrospect. I know, I know," Mother said soothingly. She gave me a sideways look. "While we're talking clichés, dare I mention, where Brock Peters is concerned, 'This, too, will pass'?"

I gave that the ignoring it deserved.

* * *

Herbert—excuse me, *Zack*—showed up promptly at three o'clock. He was wearing painfully clean sneakers (new? expensive!), clean but acceptably aged jeans, and a plaid shirt (ironed). Tucked under his left arm was Theodore, wrapped in a towel and with a wide red satin ribbon tied around his middle. In his right hand, so help me, was a bunch of garden flowers, which he thrust at my mother, not at me.

"Aunt Marge, I'm sorry about last night. I was rude and thoughtless. My mother's already pounded that fact into me, so you don't have to. My only excuse is, it's a good thing for this guy that I did go out exploring instead of coming here as I was supposed to." He held Theodore out, and Mother gazed at the turtle bemusedly.

"Isn't red satin a bit fancy?"

"It was the only thing I could find around the house that would stand in for a soft cast. We're still unpacking. I did find some special glue I have, so I patched his shell." Zack looked thoughtful. "I wonder if an

Ace bandage might be good?"

"Let's go buy him one." I hooked my hand firmly around Zack's arm.

We didn't go to the store; we went to the Collinses' to plot strategy. The house was lovely, clapboard and Jersey fieldstone, sprawling in three levels along the side of a gentle rise. There was a brook, widening into a small pond, in the backyard. "New home for Theodore, after his shell hardens," Zack said, but for now he carried the turtle into the house and deposited him in the bathtub. I raised my eyebrows.

"Aunt Lenore is going to be thrilled."

"She's used to me by now. Come down to my room. Or what's going to be my room, once I pick out new furniture." The room, on the lower level, was probably meant to be a family room. It was wood-paneled and had sliding glass doors that opened on the rear lawn. Right now it contained a mattress in the middle of the floor and a long table piled with boxes. MICROSCOPE, BUNSEN BURNER, LAB EQUIPMENT, the labels said. I blinked.

"You really are into science."

"Greatest fun I know. You wouldn't believe what you can find looking back at you through the microscope sometimes. I can't wait to have a go at the water from our pond." Zack's voice was muffled as he rummaged in the closet.

He emerged at last with a navy blue suit. "Ma's calling your mother from work to invite you all out for dinner tonight. Someplace fancy; she wants to celebrate. Is this okay to wear?"

"It looks great," I answered.

"Good. It's the only thing I haven't outgrown. I had to buy it for a cousin's wedding this spring. Make yourself comfortable, why don't you." Zack folded himself up on the mattress, and I settled, cross-legged, opposite him. "I need a bunch of new clothes. You don't think much of my style. Neither does my mother. You know what the guys around here are wearing, so how about you pick out my new stuff for me?"

And a new haircut, I thought, and different glasses. Maybe I'd better break all that to him gradually. I said instead, "Why me? Aunt Lenore may not know this neighborhood yet, but she has great taste. She's a senior buyer for a great department store. I bet she'd love it if you gave her a chance to make you over."

"Sure, she would. I bet Aunt Marge would love a chance to make *you* over. You going to give it to her?"

"Ouch."

We grinned at each other.

"Okay, I'll take you shopping. You might as well get stuff you can take to college next year. I'll do some scientific research," I said slyly. This was beginning to sound like fun.

"Fine. But remember it works both ways," Zack came back. "What are *you* going to wear tonight? How about that blue thing you had on yesterday? I liked the color."

Imagine him noticing. I perked up more. "It got pretty muddy, but I'll see what I can do."

I went home to find that Aunt Lenore had phoned and Joey had used up all the hot water. While I waited for more to accumulate, I called Michiko to report that the Collinses and Prendergasts were going out to dinner together, and that Zack had specially requested I wear my turquoise dress.

Michiko gave an elaborate sigh of relief. "At last! You're *finally* waking up from your crush on Peters!"

"I don't have a crush. And it's too soon to

say." I let my voice go dreamy. "But. . .well, maybe. . . ."

It felt weird and unfair to be putting on an act with Michiko. But Zack was right, it was the only way to go. If I could keep Michiko from meeting him till he'd had his image makeover, maybe she'd believe I really was falling for him. If Michiko could believe it, anybody could—even Brock.

Brock.

I kept thinking of him all the time I was washing the mud out of my blue dress and running it through the dryer, and getting dressed. I kept thinking about him on the way to the inn for dinner, too, but not as much, because the reality of Zack kept intruding. In the blue suit Zack, astonishingly, resembled the awkward but endearing young doctors who provide the love interest on Mother's favorite afternoon soap operas.

We had dinner in an air-conditioned dining room, at a table overlooking the terrace. As we ate shrimp cocktails, Aunt Lenore told us about the prawns and avocado she'd had on her latest buying trip to London, while Zack murmured to me about the aquatic family habits of shrimp. When we moved on to duck with sour

56

cherries, Zack started telling me about ducks, too, till I whispered to him to shut up and let me enjoy what I was eating.

There was piano music, and during and after dinner there was dancing. Dad danced with Aunt Lenore; he danced with Mother. I danced with Dad. I danced with Zack. He was right; he wasn't very good. When we'd stumbled for the fourth time and he was getting red, I took pity on him. "You've done your duty, and we've been seen together enough for the first time. If you want to sneak off for a while, I'll cover for you."

"You're a pal," Zack murmured gratefully. He tugged at his collar. "I would like to go have a look at those geese on the lawn before it gets totally dark. You want a Coke or anything? I'll bring it with me when I come in."

He cut out, and I stood by the door for a few minutes, watching the geese waddling across the inn's golf course, before going slowly back. Mother and Aunt Lenore were alone at the table now, facing toward the window, and they neither saw nor heard me coming. But I heard them.

". . . so glad if they did click," Aunt Lenore was saying wryly. "Oh, I know you think I'm being a mother hen, but I do worry. Herbie ought to have friends his own age, not just middle-aged scientists! It would be so good for him if Celia took an interest!"

"And for her," Mother said, just as ruefully. "Honestly, Lenore, I watch, and I try to keep my mouth shut. But I could just cry for her sometimes. Celia has a wonderful personality, and such a great sense of humor. And so much potential, if she'd just work on it the right way. Instead she knocks herself out to make herself look like our local teen idol's latest flame, trying to get a pat on the head like an eager puppy."

I stood, frozen. In my hot crimson solitude I heard Aunt Lenore add, with tender sadness, "Go on, Marge, say it. Like me, our first year at college, when my world revolved around What's-his-name. And all he cared about was himself and mysterious exotics, only I was plain vanilla. And you couldn't make me see. . . ."

Aunt Lenore plain vanilla? The jolt registered fleetingly, but then was gone. What was real was the pity in their voices and the searing reflection of myself that those words presented.

Trying to get a pat on the head like an eager puppy. Was *that* the way I looked—to my family, to Michiko, even to Brock?

In my misery I heard my mother's voice quicken, heard her whispering to my godmother, "Look, Lenore. That's him!" And I followed their gaze out the window to a terrace table where a dark-blond figure was bending forward to look with admiration into the eyes of a slim, blond girl in vivid silk. Brock. And Laurie Malone.

I wasn't like her. I could never be like her. Celia, with the great personality, the great sense of humor. Celia, the puppy dog. Celia, who was terrific at putting up posters, writing publicity stories, working on committees, but who had no glamour. Celia, who was plain vanilla.

Celia, who probably wouldn't get to first base with Brock in spite of this charade Zack and I had cooked up. Admit it, I told myself brutally, with deep shame. You thought Zack was a dog. In spite of the nice things about him, you thought he was worse off than you. And it isn't true. Because Zack likes himself just the way he is.

And right now I did not.

I was terribly glad the room was dim, because everything I was feeling had to show in my face. I was terribly glad Zack had not been there to hear. But when I turned, after wiping eyes that had suddenly stung and blurred, there he was, motionless, a tall glass of soda in each hand.

He had heard every word. But he never mentioned it. Not then. Not ever.

FIVE

August was approaching. Oakdale grew hot and humid, and everybody who could took off for elsewhere. Brock and his parents went white-water rafting. The Kimuras visited Michiko's aunt and uncle on the coast of Maine. Aunt Lenore was immersed in her new job and new house and couldn't get away, but Zack left for a science conference at the University of Michigan. He would return the day after my family took off for our annual four weeks at Cape May, New Jersey. Two postcards came to me from Zack before we left. One, almost undecipherable in small, packed handwriting, effervesced with excitement about the conference. The other, obviously for public consumption, said in large clear printing, HAVING A GREAT TIME. WISH YOU WERE HERE. SEE YOU SOON.

I took it over to show Aunt Lenore, and she said, "Hmm," exactly as my mother had. I turned red, of course, and she chuckled. "Don't be embarrassed! I'm *not* trying to cook up a serious romance! I do have that much self-restraint. If you can get my son to become even a halfway social animal, I'll be more than happy. In fact, I'll give you anything your heart desires."

"I wish you'd teach me how to stop being plain vanilla."

I didn't intend to say that. The words just popped out, probably because I was sticky hot and my nose was peeling, and Aunt Lenore looked so cool and serene. She sat up straight on the off-white sofa, and her eyes were startled.

"What made you say that?"

I turned redder yet, remembering. "I— heard somewhere that's what you used to call yourself. But you're not plain now!"

My godmother chuckled. "I just grew up,

that's all. And you're not plain, Celia, not with that gorgeous hair."

"It's a prize pain," I said grimly. "It frizzes up in this weather."

"Cut it."

"And nothing goes with it, especially my sunburn! I look like—like pumpkin pie with strawberry ice cream!"

Aunt Lenore threw back her head and laughed aloud. But she sobered quickly. "I'm sorry! I can tell it's no joke to you. You're so clever with words, I couldn't help cracking up. No wonder you're an editor on your school paper."

"I'd swap more than a few bylines to look like you," I said, and meant it.

She shook her head. "We're totally different types. What you're really talking about is that I've found my type, and you haven't yet. I admit, working in fashion merchandising gave me an edge, but everything I've learned, you can."

"Teach me."

"You're serious, aren't you?" Aunt Lenore gave me a long look, but her voice was matter-of-fact. "I can tell you three things that would make a lot of difference. Get a good haircut. I'll take you to my stylist, if you want. Stay out of the sun; your skin's too fragile for it, and too much exposure's a health risk, anyway. And pick clothes that will play up your hair, not compete with it."

I blinked. "I thought that's what I *was* doing!"

"Let me show you." She steered me to a gilt-framed mirror. "See how that bright blue top drains all the color from your face? Any bright shade would—vivid green, purple, turquoise."

I winced, remembering the turquoise dress. "I read those colors were good for redheads," I said defensively.

"They are, with green or blue eyes. But your eyes are brown. When you wear those colors, your clothes and all that hair start competing for attention. Your features fade away. Nobody sees *you* at all."

"Oh, they see sunburn," I said brightly, being the comedian again.

"Right. But I thought we already agreed you didn't want that." She pulled a creamy sweater from her shoulders and draped it to cover me from the throat down. "Plain vanilla, again," she said dryly, "but take a look."

She was holding my hair up off my neck,

bunched in her hand so it looked like a wavy cap. The vanilla color made it look like polished copper and gentled the burned flush in my skin. "Add some brown mascara, and maybe a smudge of brown or taupe around the eyes, and the results could be pretty spectacular, don't you think?"

"I can't believe it," I said slowly.

"Oh, you can. If you like, I'll make an appointment for the haircut and bring you in the store for a makeup demonstration." Aunt Lenore caught herself. "Sorry. I didn't mean to come on like a mother. You have a perfectly good one of your own. It's just the stylist in me taking over."

"That's okay." I took a deep breath, feeling light-headed. "You're practically family, and I can take advice better from somebody who's not my parent. Just as Herbert probably can," I added daringly.

"It's Zack now, so I gather from his cards. I rather like it." Aunt Lenore smiled back at me. "Does that mean you want me to make the appointments for you?"

"For the haircut. Let's let the face go until the sunburn fades." Aunt Lenore's store was in a nearby mall, and I didn't relish the thought of being a guinea pig in full view of any wandering shoppers from Oakdale High.

By pulling strings, Aunt Lenore was able to get me an appointment the evening before my family left for the Jersey shore. She went with me, to lend moral support and supervision. With great self-control I kept my eyes and mouth shut till the job was done.

We went back to the Elephant afterward, and my family's reaction was gratifying. Mother's jaw dropped. Dad stared, and stared again, and a nostalgic look came into his eyes. "You look like my mother did when I was a little kid." He went upstairs and returned with the locket that was a memento of the grandmother who'd died before I was born. "You're old enough to have this now."

I gazed at the hand-tinted miniature of a dark-eyed young woman, her cap of copper hair waving softly onto her cheekbones as mine now did.

Of course Joey, looking me over, had a few derisive things to say. But I ignored him magnificently.

The next morning we left for Cape May, all four of us—six, counting the girls. Traffic was bumper-to-bumper on the parkway, and Missy and Susie drove us crazy, climbing back and forth to look out windows. But once the four-hour ride was done, we settled happily into our regular summer routine. With two exceptions. The girls ate too much sand and weeds and upchucked on the carpet for two days. And I ate a bad hot dog on the Wildwood boardwalk and wound up in the hospital emergency room at two in the morning.

I do not recommend having food poisoning as the pleasantest way to a svelte figure, but it worked. Between that experience and the humid weather, I was totally turned off food, and I dropped ten pounds in as many days. I also dropped my sunburn. I did a lot of swimming, but when I wasn't under the waves I did my lying around under a beach umbrella, making plans for the first issue of the *Oakleaf.* I bought myself a wide-brimmed sun hat, and it started getting me noticed, particularly when I had the girls along. It's hard to fade into the woodwork when you stroll along the boardwalk attached to a German shepherd, a Sheltie, and a cream-colored Guatemalan hat a yard wide.

The day Susie decided to swipe the hat and run with it into the waves, two lifeguards and three college-jock types interrupted their volleyball game to catch her, and after that the Prendergasts had a permanent floating card game going on under our beach umbrella that attracted plenty of handsome young men. It was definitely the most rewarding vacation of my life.

We drove home the Thursday before Labor Day in order to escape the weekend traffic. It was very late at night when we reached the Elephant, but early the next morning the telephone started ringing. Aunt Lenore called Mother to report that Zack had gotten himself a part-time internship at Dynachem, and to suggest a picnic in their backyard on Labor Day. Laurie Malone phoned to warn me she was calling a meeting of the *Oakleaf* staff right after school on our first day back. "And come with ideas! Labor Day's late this year, so we'll have only two weeks to get the first issue out. I thought we'd make it a sports special. How does that sound to you?"

"It sounds great. I've made a list of possibilities for the feature pages."

"Oh, good! I really hope we can have a lot

of group participation this year. Not so much—you know." Yes, I did. Last year's editor in chief had been a do-it-all-yourself whiz kid who'd frequently bitten off more than he could chew. He'd doled out assignments late, made constant changes without telling anybody, and rewritten everything. Laurie had been features editor then, and I'd been one of the reporters. "And I sure hope we can be better organized this year!" Laurie laughed. "I'm really glad you're an editor, Celia. You're so good at things like that. See you Wednesday, okay?"

My next caller was Michiko. "I've been trying to reach you for two hours," she said plaintively. "What were you doing, talking to lover boy? Or should I say, one of the lover boys?"

"Cute, real cute. Remind me not to tell you about the Prendergast Cape May Daily Card Game Competition. The past hour and a half hasn't been my fault. Joey's been busy plugging himself into mini-league soccer. How was Maine?"

"Oh," Michiko said lightly, "not so bad. I finally learned the fingering for that Mozart concertino. David showed it to me."

"David?"

"Just a boy I met. He plays viola and goes to Juilliard. Remind me not to tell you about him, either." Michiko paused for a second. "Brock's back. I saw him at the carnival last night. Not with Laurie. With a new girl, Terrie something. It looks as if he's going to play the field this year."

I chuckled. "When hasn't he? Officially or otherwise. I'm just glad I'm not a part of it."

"*Ohhh?*" Michiko inquired. When I didn't bite, she went on, "Want to go down to the carnival tonight? Or do you have plans?"

"I was planning to see you," I answered truthfully. "The carnival sounds fine."

I certainly did want a planning session with Zack, but I had no idea yet what he was up to. Besides, the great Prendergast/Collins deal had been his idea; the next move was up to him.

The carnival was an annual affair, sponsored by the Lions Club to raise money for charity. The Lions Club also presented annual Citizenship Award scholarships to one boy and one girl in each graduating class. It wasn't the money, though that was considerable, that made these awards so coveted: They were based on the votes of the entire senior class, the faculty, and a panel of civic leaders. Brock would undoubtedly be a recipient this year; I would dearly love to get one in two years, when I'd be a senior.

Still, it wasn't the fund-raising that brought the whole town out for the carnival each year; it was the fun, and the chance to be a child again. Where else could we eat cotton candy and toss wet sponges at our principal's face? It might not occur to Zack to show up there tonight, but Brock surely would.

Ordinarily, I'd wear jeans, but my jeans were loose now, and all my tops were the colors Aunt Lenore had called competitive. I thought long and hard and put on a T-shirt dress the color of vanilla ice cream. Also brown mascara, which I'd bought while at the shore.

I set off for the carnival as dusk was falling. I was accompanied by Joey, which had not been part of the original idea. He just wanted to go so badly, and my parents had an emergency involving a leaking pipe, so I relented.

"You can go off on your own once you're past the ticket booth, young man. But you're not to go outside the carnival grounds, and you're to remember when and where your sister says to meet her, understand?" Dad said firmly.

Joey nodded vigorously, with an ominously angelic expression, and we set out. Michiko was waiting for me at the carnival grounds, and she did a double take. "What have you *done* to yourself?"

"I had food poisoning," I said smugly. "It works wonders."

Michiko shook her head. "It's not just the weight. It's something else. What is—"

"Later," I interrupted with a significant look at my brother. Fortunately, Joey was too much in a hurry to get away from me to offer any embarrassing explanations of his own. I bought our tickets, told him to be at the ice-cream stand at nine o'clock sharp, and we split up.

"Hold the story till later. I'd rather hear it in private, anyway," Michiko said. "You look great!"

"I'll tell you about it when I hear about the viola player," I said blandly.

Michiko ignored that. "Brock's here. With Laurie. I thought maybe she'd started going with someone else over the summer, but I guess not." She gave me a sideways look. "Is your friend—what's his name, Herbert?— going to be here?"

"Zack? I haven't any idea. We still haven't

72

managed to meet up with each other. Except by mail, while I was away. You know how it is," I said airily.

Michiko giggled. "Stop looking like the cat that ate the canary. On second thought, don't stop. It might give Great God Peters something to think about."

"Forget Brock. He's not what's on my mind tonight," I retorted untruthfully. I locked my arm through hers and we started making the rounds of the carnival attractions, acting silly.

It was nearly dark, and the Ferris wheel lights were glowing like jewels against the sky, when Michiko nudged me. "I know you're not interested, but there he is."

Brock and Laurie Malone were coming toward us, their arms around each other.

Two months ago I'd have waited for them to speak first. Tonight I sang out, "Hi, you two!"

"Hi, Celia!" It was Laurie who said that; Brock just looked. His expression was blank at first, then slightly puzzled.

He was just about to speak when a male voice some ways behind him bellowed out, *"Cele!"* in obvious delight.

A blond giant was bearing down on us, a

giant with sun-bleached hair that dazzled like silver under the carnival lights. With aviator glasses, and a haircut straight off one of the most popular TV heroes, and an Oakdale Lions Club sweatshirt, which happens to be very "in." "Cele!" he repeated happily, ignoring everyone else around. "I've been trying to reach you on the phone every five minutes since I got home from work, but your line's been busy!"

It took me a full sixty seconds to realize that it was Zack Collins.

SIX

———✦———

I performed introductions in a daze. Brock and Zack shook hands. Zack hardly paid attention—it was obvious to all he wanted to get me off alone. Not bad strategy, I applauded mentally. Brock and Laurie took themselves off, and Michiko tactfully did likewise. Zack put his hand under my elbow and started hurrying me along.

"Can we go somewhere and feed our faces? Not here. We need to talk."

"I *was* supposed to be doing the carnival with my best friend," I said dryly.

"Is that who that was?" Zack asked blankly.

"I'm sorry. All I was thinking about was—"
Then he did a double take. "Brock Peters?
Isn't that the guy—"

"It is. And the girl with him is the chief
competition."

Zack, thus reminded, stopped to
reconsider. An appreciative smile spread
across his face. "She certainly is spectacular."

"You noticed that."

"I'm not totally blind," Zack said with
dignity. He stared at me up and down,
considering. "You look good, too. You've
changed."

"That's right. Speaking of which—"

Somebody jostled us, and Zack said
decisively, "We can't talk here. Come on."

"We can't leave. I'm supposed to keep an
eye on Joey."

"Okay, we'll talk after we dump him at
home," Zack agreed. We started making the
rounds of the carnival. Pretty soon we
encountered Joey, who was searching for me
to con me out of cash. Zack and he went up
in the Ferris wheel together. Then we all
went through the Haunted House, and Joey
and Zack both made awful faces back at the
scary figures.

"You're both idiots," I told them severely.

But I couldn't keep from smiling.

We threw sponges at Mr. McPhail, the principal. We threw balls at bottles. We ate popcorn, and soft ice cream, and cotton candy. Finally, we deposited Joey back home at the Elephant.

"Can't I see my girl for a while without a chaperone?" Zack asked good-naturedly when Joey started to protest.

"Is Celia your girl? Oh boy, oh boy!" Joey crowed.

"That," I said when we'd left, "was as good as printing an announcement in the paper!"

"That's the general idea, isn't it?" Zack inquired amiably. "Where do you want to go?"

"Anywhere, so long as I don't have to eat anything. That cotton candy was the limit."

So we walked back to the Dynachem headquarters and sat down on the bank of the stream, smiling at each other.

"How was the shore?" Zack asked.

"Terrific. I gather the science seminar was, too. Whatever prompted you to go TV macho?" When Zack looked blank, I added patiently, "The haircut." I named the show and its detective hero. Zack shook his head.

"Never saw it. You said I needed a haircut.

A couple of guys at the seminar wore their hair like this. They're both good, sensible scientists, and they had tons of girls around them all the time, so I figured this was the way to go."

"And the glasses?"

"I broke my old ones, and I liked these," Zack said simply.

I looked at him, long arms looped around long legs, and marveled. Zack the scientist, without even thinking about it, had played a long shot and had picked exactly right. "Did you do anything about clothes?" I asked warily.

"You said you'd take care of those," Zack pointed out.

I needed new ones, too, the extent of which I hadn't yet broken to my parents. "We'd better go down to the shopping outlets in the Meadowlands. The highways will be jammed till Labor Day weekend's over, and school starts Wednesday." We settled on Tuesday. Zack would borrow his mother's car. We would *not* take parents.

It was after midnight before it occurred to us we should go home. Zack apologized for keeping me out so late, said he'd see me the next day, and left. Mother, who'd been waiting up for me on the front porch, looked dazed.

"You *told* me to make him feel at home here," I said neatly, and went to bed before she could ask questions.

It was a delicious weekend. On Saturday Michiko and I played tennis, and she told me about David. I told her bits and pieces about Zack, while acting as if there was a lot more I wasn't telling, which was the plain truth.

"You bringing him to the Pops concert Monday night?" Michiko asked.

"I might. Tell me more about David. When are you going to be seeing him again?" I was starting to feel uncomfortable about holding out.

On Saturday afternoon I went to the bookstore and bought a paperback about men's clothing and dressing for success. I suspected it would take solid research to convince Zack some of his ingrained habits had to go. I learned for certain they were ingrained when he showed up to take me to the movies Saturday night, looking like a nerd from the neck down.

"That shirt," I told him firmly, "has to go. Also the little plastic pen-and-pencil holder in your pocket. And those shoes."

"What's wrong with them?" Zack asked, hurt.

"They're the color of a pumpkin and they look like they were made out of old tires! Great for wading in the muck for turtles—how is Theodore, by the way?—but not for dates or school."

"Make me out a list so I'll remember," Zack said with a sigh. "Theodore's fine. His shell isn't as thick as it should be, though. I think he has some kind of genetic deficiency."

We spent the rest of the evening having a romantic conversation about the DNA of aquatic species.

On Labor Day our two families had cold roast chicken and corn on the cob and apple slump on a picnic table by the stream at the bottom of the Collins garden, and afterward we all took folding chairs to the municipal field to watch the fireworks and hear the Pops concert. Up in the band shell, in the violin section, Michiko looked different, delicate and older in the long black dress she always wore for concerts. Her face was grave as she bent over her instrument. But when we met her later, her impish smile appeared.

"Are you going anywhere now that the concert's over?" she asked.

Zack looked at me. Apparently, he felt in need of guidance and was waiting for a clue. At the same moment Laurie Malone said, "Hi, Celia!" She was with Brock, and a couple of other jocks, and two girls I knew vaguely from the school paper. Laurie was smiling, she looked genuinely glad to see me, and Brock—

. There was an expression I couldn't quite identify in Brock's eyes. He was looking straight at me, and I was wearing the vanilla ice-cream dress.

All at once I heard my own voice saying gaily, "You guys want to come back to our place? We have a freezer full of ice cream, and Mom made a cake!"

"I'll go get David," Michiko said, dashing off.

David. David Perlman had come all the way from Long Island to hear Michiko play—a little item Michiko hadn't told me about. Hmmm, I thought.

"We'd love to come," Laurie said. "Is this open house?"

"Sure!" I said recklessly. "Spread the word!"

We ended up with about thirty kids sprawled on wicker furniture or porch rockers or front steps. Joey and the girls freaked out, Dad enjoyed himself thoroughly, and Mother and Aunt Lenore looked bemused.

Once I caught Brock watching me with that same expression—faintly puzzled, faintly challenging. Then I felt another pair of eyes on me, and my own were drawn involuntarily toward them. Zack was draped across the porch railing behind Brock's back. When my gaze met his, he winked.

* * *

The next morning, as soon as the commuter rush was past, Zack and I took off for the discount clothing outlets in the Meadowlands. To my pleasant surprise, Aunt Lenore's car was a convertible, and the top was down. Zack drove, and I gave him a lecture on the Importance of Having the Right Image.

"Clothing's not only covering, or temperature regulation, or fashion. It's really a uniform that shows what group you belong to." This was the gospel according to the researcher whose book I'd studied.

Zack, while willing to go along to get his mother off his back, thought it was funny. "What's so important about being part of a group?"

"*Everybody* needs to belong somewhere! If you don't understand that yet, Zack Collins, *you're* the dimwit." I glanced at him sitting there with a smug smile on his face, and a little imp prompted me to go scientific. "It's a . . . a tribal thing. It connects us with our roots, and shows our loyalty to collective standards, and where we fit in and what can be expected of us. That's why uniforms are just as important in a school or a job as in the army or on a team." I gave him a sideways look. "What would you think if I showed up to hunt for marine specimens wearing high-heeled shoes?"

"I'd think you were a jerk. Okay, I get your point. Just give me a list," Zack said with exaggerated patience, "and I'll follow it!"

I had several lists. One was for an entire new wardrobe for Zack. One, pretty nearly as extensive, was for me. Dad had come through magnificently with a wad of cash. Another list, patterned on the kind of instructions Mother wrote out for Joey when he went to camp, told Zack what he should wear with what for specific occasions.

There was also a list, otherwise known as Basic Characteristics of a Nerd, of taboos to be avoided at any cost. I decided I'd better handle that one with a lot of tact. Somewhat to my surprise, I found myself feeling fiercely mother hen. Zack was funny and kind and turning into a good friend, and I was not going to have him written off by others as a weirdo, just because he was a babe in the woods about our social customs!

I'd had grave doubts about Zack as a shopping partner, but I got a big surprise. Zack behaved like a lamb. He bought what I picked out for him without argument, and he had useful comments when I consulted him about clothes for me.

I was feeling pretty good as we started for home. I had just acquired a whole wardrobe two sizes smaller, in shades of cream through tawny, with side excursions into taupe and olive green. We were cruising the highway in a convertible with the top down, and the September sun was shining.

I leaned back and relaxed, and inquired about Theodore, and for the rest of the trip home Zack treated me to a dissertation on the mating habits of swamp turtles. It was pretty hilarious, and I had a very good time.

It wasn't till I was getting ready for bed that I looked in the mirror at my not-yet-familiar new reflection, and my blessings started to enumerate themselves to me.

Tomorrow was the first day of my sophomore year in high school. I was going to sail into school with, apparently, a brand-new boyfriend who looked exactly right. And who, as an added bonus, was a clever collaborator and down-to-earth friend.

Zack thought I looked good. He might have the world's worst taste, but he was a male, and far from stupid. He was rational and logical, and he rationally thought my turning Brock Peters on, and keeping him turned on, was practically guaranteed.

And all because of Zack himself and his incredible, wacky "deal."

I felt a profound gratitude and liking for Zack as I crawled into bed. But it was Brock Peters's deeply tanned, mysteriously alluring face I saw in my mind's eye as I fell asleep.

SEVEN

On Wednesday morning I sailed into Oakdale High School in my new cocoa-and-olive paisley skirt and cream-colored shirt, and before I'd gotten up the stairs to homeroom I knew this year was definitely going to be different.

It wasn't just seeing Zack towering at the far end of the hall, waving to me. It was something in the air. It was the looks on other people's faces. It was having Laurie Malone and other seniors hail me by name to say something about the *Oakleaf* or about what a neat time they'd had at my house the other night. It was having classmates—not just Michiko and Beth Lemoine and Dorothy Sheridan, who are part of my regular lunch group, but others who just knew me slightly—looking pleased to see me. And it was hearing a subdued but unmistakable whistle coming from Mike Rafferty as I passed him. I spun around, disbelieving, and he grinned and waved.

"Lookin' good, kid! Lookin' good!"

"Let's hope you look as good at football practice this afternoon," I answered pertly.

He laughed. "Come take a look, why don't you."

"Mmmm . . . maybe."

I encountered Laurie Malone again as I was hurrying down the stairs from chem lab to the cafeteria at lunchtime. "Don't forget the *Oakleaf* meeting, Celia. Three o'clock, Room 213. You ready with those ideas you promised?"

I waved my notebook at her.

As always, there were more people trying to get to the cafeteria lunch counters than the room could accommodate. The line snaked out into the hall, blocking lockers. "About time we had a bigger cafeteria," I grumbled audibly, attaching myself to the tail end of the line.

Behind me a familiar voice, with a hint of a laugh in it, responded, "That would be a good campaign for the *Oakleaf* this year, wouldn't it? Think about it. Is the time ripe for Celia Prendergast, girl crusader?"

It was Brock.

"It could be ripe for a *woman* crusading journalist, if that's what you're trying so gallantly to say," I retorted with irony. It was incredible. I was standing here talking to Brock Peters and pulling out the kind of lines that came naturally when I was with Michiko or my family. "*If* she believes in the issue. Are you planning to campaign for Student Council president on a school expansion platform, Mr. Peters?"

"I've always looked at the big picture," Brock replied in the same tone. He leaned one elbow against the wall next to us and grinned. "How about it, Celia? You going to work for my campaign again this year? Providing I decide to run, of course!"

"Of course," I echoed dryly. "Somehow I can't see you sitting on the sidelines. It's not your style."

"My old man's always told me, 'If you've got it, use it,'" Brock agreed. He glanced ahead and nudged me. "Wake up, crusader!

The line's moving."

I moved obediently, and then two loud-mouthed freshmen cut in line between us, and we didn't have a chance to talk anymore.

Michiko and Dorothy were already at our regular table. Michiko pushed my chair out toward me with her toes. "How's your little waif doing in the wilds of Oakdale High?" she asked me.

"I don't know. I haven't seen him except across the wasteland of the second floor this morning. He has all senior classes."

"What waif?" Dorothy demanded. And then, in tones of pleased discovery, "Who is that?"

That was Zack, barreling toward us like an adolescent German shepherd. His tray was laden.

"Put your eyes back in your head," I advised Dorothy. "I saw him first." I pulled out a chair and Zack folded up into it.

Rare is the boy, especially a new one, who'd attach himself to a "female table" in our cafeteria. Zack either didn't know that or he didn't care. He was attracting notice anyway; first, because of his size, and second, because he stood up, put two fingers between his lips, and whistled. "Yo, Bruce!"

A tall, dark senior whom I knew by sight put on the brakes, broke into a smile, and loped over. "You guys know Bruce Hammond? We work together at Dynachem." Zack looked around the table. "Celia's lost her power of speech, so I'll introduce myself. Zack Collins. Senior."

"Dorothy Sheridan. Sophomore."

"Beth Lemoine. Sophomore."

"Michiko Kimura. But you already know that, don't you?" she murmured, wickedly demure.

"This clown has just moved here from the Midwest," I explained. "Would you believe I'm stuck with him because his mom's my godmother and she wants her little lost sheep to have a guide dog?"

This was taken in the spirit it deserved. "Some 'stuck'!" Michiko whispered in my ear. What she said aloud was, "Some little lost sheep! You seem to be doing pretty well for yourself." She cast a sardonic glance at the arm Zack had draped around my shoulder.

"I am, aren't I?" Zack agreed smugly.

Was he overdoing the act? I wondered. I looked around, and three tables away I beheld Brock sitting in the exact same pose with Laurie. I gave Zack a sharp kick in the ankle, which he ignored.

"Going out for basketball?" Dorothy asked, batting her eyelashes.

"I'm not much into sports, unless you count marathon cycling or racquetball. When I'm outdoors, I'd rather do stuff more worthwhile than chasing a ball around." I made a note to remind Zack basketball was an indoor game, and to make him a list of Comments Not to Make. Meanwhile, Zack was going blithely on. "You guys have any kind of environmental club around here?"

There were general groans. "That's about the dullest club on campus," Beth explained. "Only the nerds belong, and they never do anything." Even Bruce agreed, and recommended the Science or Civic Action clubs instead.

From then on, the advice being handed to Zack degenerated into silliness. The cafeteria rocked with our mirth. People at other tables turned around and smiled at us, and by the time lunch period was over, I had the satisfaction of knowing Zack was well on the way to assimilation.

That left me free to enjoy the rest of the day myself. And I *did* enjoy it. After lunch was advanced art, which was always fun. Then came Problems of American Democracy, which did not thrill me, but at least Michiko was a fellow sufferer. And last period was study hall, in the cafeteria. Brock had study hall, too, and he sat opposite me.

"Coming to watch football practice this afternoon?" he whispered when the monitor wasn't near.

I shook my head. "I have an *Oakleaf* staff meeting. So does Laurie," I added deliberately. Brock pulled a mock-tragic face.

"How am I going to do well with nobody to inspire me?"

"Oh, you'll manage!"

I couldn't believe myself, trading smart remarks with him like this. I never could before, though Michiko had often lectured me on my lack of confidence. I blessed Zack and his brainstorm for having provided it.

The dismissal bell rang, and I made for the stairs. In Room 213 the *Oakleaf* staff—editor in chief; news, sports, photography, and features editors; plus business manager—draped themselves at, on, or over desks. Laurie herself perched on the teacher's desk, looking determined and excited.

"I really want to make this year's *Oakleaf* special. We have a real chance to get our teeth into things for a change!"

There were muffled groans. "With Blauvelt on our tails?" Everybody knew what Pete Bayer, the news editor, meant. Ms. Blauvelt was a dear, but her main objectives for the paper were that it be grammatically correct and not rock any boats.

"You mean you haven't heard?" Laurie asked, surprised. "Blauvelt decided out of the blue last week to take early retirement and move to North Carolina."

"Who's our new faculty adviser?" I asked.

Laurie's eyes twinkled. "Hang on to your hats, kids. It's Stephen Oliver."

There was a reverent silence. Stephen Oliver was in his late thirties and a former professional journalist. He believed that newspapers, even school newspapers, should get involved in issues. He was the shining light of the Oakdale English department, and last year he had been New Jersey's Teacher of the Year. There was hope the *Oakleaf* could now get away with more than it had in the past.

Walter Joyce, the sports editor, looked around. "Where is Oliver, anyway?"

"He thought we should have a chance to get started on our own. He'll be here next time." Laurie grasped her clipboard firmly. "Before we start brainstorming, let's get some policy matters settled. We've *got* to get our issues out on time this year!"

There was a chorus of complaints about the printers, which the business manager, Jo Egan, shouted down. "I know they're awful, but they give us the best price. The school board only gives us so much money for our fun and games. And if you think I can come up with more advertising, forget it. It's hard enough to con even the freshmen into going around selling ads!"

"We'll just have to plan on turning the copy in to the printers a week early." Laurie sighed. "What I'd really like would be to publish every other week, not once a marking period. Particularly now that we've got Oliver and could go after solid stories. But there's just no way."

That's when lightning struck. "Yes, there is," I exclaimed involuntarily.

Every head in the room swiveled toward me. "Not on our budget," Jo said kindly.

"There is if we print the paper ourselves, here in the school. The art department just bought a photo-offset printer." I swung around to Laurie. "You were in art class. You heard Fontanazza bragging about getting the school board to finally okay the purchase! Why couldn't we get the Art Club to do our printing for us? Maybe work on layout, too! I bet they'd give us an issue every other week for a lot less money than we're paying our current printers. The Art Club treasury's as deprived as ours is."

You could feel a current of excitement flowing through the room. "Typesetting?" somebody asked.

"We have a computer department, don't we?" I retorted. "Let's get them in on this."

"Maybe the business classes could sell ads!"

"If the *Oakleaf* comes out more often, and covers real news, more businesses may want in."

"I'll talk to my dad. He's in the Chamber of Commerce."

The idea was really catching fire.

Laurie rapped on the desk. "Okay, okay! The first thing is to find out if we can self-publish. Jo, find out whether we're locked into a contract with the printers. Celia, you talk to Mr. Fontanazza about the Art Club."

I gulped. "Doesn't this have to—go through channels?"

"We *are* the channel. I know Oliver will be for it. He's always wanted the *Oakleaf* to turn into a real paper. Printing here was your idea, Celia, so you follow through. Everybody agreed we move ahead on this?" Laurie asked. There was a chorus of assent. "Okay, now let's get down to the nitty-gritty of the first issue. Pete, what's your lead story?"

Pete Bayer, news editor, grinned. "This is, if we pull it off. Plus the centralized computer system the school put in during the summer."

"Celia?"

I cleared my throat. "I was thinking of a feature on the people expected to be the stars in sports this year."

"Muscling in on my territory, Prendergast?" Walter Joyce inquired, grinning.

"Not at all," I retorted neatly. "You'll be concentrating on our football lineup, won't you?" He nodded. "I was thinking of doing a profile of *every* sport, sort of an overview of how important sports are on the Oakdale scene. The sports page always concentrates on football in the fall, so the football stars are automatically the big deal. People in other sports don't get the limelight till later in the year, if at all. I want to cover the whole picture in one big spread, including activities that don't usually get much coverage, like intramurals, and archery, and the girls' basketball team!"

I sat back, breathless. Jo winked at me. She was on that basketball team. "I think it's a great idea," she said aloud. The idea carried.

"You're going to have some job doing all those interviews *and* getting them written in two weeks," Laurie told me as the meeting broke up. "I didn't want to say anything in front of the others, but our features writers are awfully weak this year. We're having that open meeting for new members Monday, so maybe some bright prospects will turn up. But you're apt to be stuck with a bunch of inexperienced freshmen. I'll do a couple of interviews for you, if you need me."

I struggled with selfishness and said, with what I hoped was the right lightness, "You want to interview Brock?"

"Why don't you do that one yourself?" Laurie asked, surprising me. "You know him pretty well after working on his election campaigns. Anyway, we wouldn't want

Superstar getting the idea the *Oakleaf* editor in chief was his personal groupie, would we?"

Darn Aunt Lenore and her no-sunning edict! If I were sunburned, I wouldn't have worried whether the heat I felt showed as an embarrassing blush. I achieved a laugh. "You *are* going with the guy, aren't you?" I asked, carefully casual.

"Going out with him, yes. *Going* with him, no. I don't want to get really serious with any one person while I'm in high school." Laurie turned serious. "My sister did. She went with one boy all through high school. After graduation they were half a continent apart, and she was miserable her first two years in college. I don't want that to happen to me."

All at once the room seemed brighter. My spirits spiraled even higher when Laurie added, "Those were some great ideas you came out with today. Looks like I was right to pick you for my features editor."

"*You* picked me?"

Laurie looked blank. "What did you think, you dodo? Oh, sure, Blauvelt had veto power. But I said loud and clear I'd be editor in chief only if I could pick my own staff."

So I hadn't been as invisible as I'd thought.

"I knew you'd be a good worker and a good writer," Laurie was saying. "I didn't know you'd turn out to be a good organizer and salesperson, too!"

"Neither did I," I murmured giddily. I made my way out of the now silent school building with a lot to think about.

It had been a long meeting. Although this was only the beginning of September, the sky was already turning the cool blue of twilight. The football players were still scrimmaging on the field.

It really was a more direct line to my house if I walked past the football field. At least that's what I told myself. I reached the fence just as the team was breaking up to head for the locker room.

Brock walked over and gave me his crooked smile. "Came to give me that inspiration, after all? Too bad you didn't get here sooner. I could have used it."

He looked tired and hot, and his hands were skinned. "Bad game?" I asked.

"Not a game, just tackling practice. I thought I'd kept myself in shape, but I guess I didn't. I wish we had more time before the first game!"

"You'll be ready," I said sympathetically.

"This is going to be a great year for the team, I just know it!" I said "for the team." I meant "for you."

"Thanks," Brock said. "Right now we can use all the support we can get." It wasn't like him to sound like that. Something must have really gone wrong at practice.

"Don't you, of all people, give in to preseason blues, just when I've been planning a whole feature spread on this year's sports stars!" I said teasingly. "Why, I'm even going to write the piece on you myself!"

I wasn't flirting, honestly. I was truly trying to make Brock feel better. And Brock took it that way. He said, more soberly than I'd ever heard him speak before, "Thanks. That's great." Then he took off his helmet and straightened, and the old Brock was back, carefree, charming. "Listen, Celia! I told you I wanted to get together with you— talk about my objectives for the year, and stuff. There's no law against an *Oakleaf* editor and an Oakdale captain having fun at the same time, is there? Or would that jeopardize your journalistic impartiality?"

"I don't think so," I murmured dizzily.

"Then how about going out with me Friday night?"

My mind—and, let's face it, the rest of me, too—shouted *yes!* Then I remembered that I'd promised Zack I'd go with him to a special exhibition at the Museum of Natural History that night. More to the point, I remembered what Zack had said. Brock was used to having girls come running when he called. What would catch his attention, and hold it, was a girl who didn't.

"Oh, I'm sorry," I said, and I achieved exactly the right tone of mild regret. "I already have a date for Friday. And this Saturday's taken, too. Can I take a raincheck?"

"For when?" Brock asked, exactly as he was supposed to.

And I said, as I also was supposed to, "I don't know right now. I'll have to check my calendar. Call me, okay?"

"You got it," Brock said. I thought he meant it.

"Don't forget!" I said lightly. And I walked away.

Afterward, of course, I could have kicked myself. But I'd had the guts to take the gamble. I could be proud of that. I just hoped it was a gamble I would win.

EIGHT

After that day, things started happening so swiftly I scarcely had time to think.

I talked to Mr. Fontanazza about the commercial art classes printing the *Oakleaf* on the new equipment, and he said yes. The Art Club said yes. The Computer Club thought that setting the type for the *Oakleaf*, and getting paid for it, would be far-out. The business department climbed on the bandwagon, too.

The first biweekly issue of the *Oakleaf* came out the Friday afternoon before our first football game. Laurie had been right—we had a bunch of green kids to work on it.

So it had been a hassle, but it had been fun. And it would probably get easier. The paper was distributed in the cafeteria during lunch periods. It carried Pete's front-page story about going biweekly, and Laurie's editorial promising that this year the *Oakleaf* would go boldly into territory hitherto off-limits. By three-fifteen, when I left the school grounds, five additional upperclassmen had expressed interest in joining the features department's writing staff.

"How about you?" I asked Zack that night as we stood in line for the movies. We'd amended our arrangement to cover one date per weekend until further notice, with our taking turns deciding what that date would be. The movie had been my idea. Zack was suffering through it because it was an adventure film that promised special effects involving water creatures.

Zack, on the subject of the *Oakleaf*, shook his head. "I'm no writer! Anyway, I won't have time for both the Environmental Club and that, besides working part-time for Dynachem."

I wrinkled my nose. "Are you still determined to get into that—that bunch of nonachievement?"

"Maybe I can make it achieve something," Zack said reasonably. "Are you still determined to be noticeable?"

I turned red, and he relented. "You're doing okay. Everybody's giving you credit for turning the *Oakleaf* around this year. Going biweekly and getting other school clubs involved was brilliant."

I blushed even more, this time from pleasure. "It wasn't just me! Mr. Oliver's the one who made it possible. And Laurie was already thinking about more issues and more involvement. I just figured out how."

"Yeah, Laurie has good brains along with good looks," Zack said approvingly. "But don't underestimate your contribution. You saw the problem, evaluated the options, and zeroed right in on the solution. And implemented it. That's being a leader, not a follower."

"Will you shut up?" I begged in a whisper. We were in a long ticket line, and Zack's voice carried.

Zack laughed, but obligingly lowered his voice. "As I was saying, you don't need me on the *Oakleaf.* You're doing fine without me. I read the interview you wrote on Peters."

Brock and I had had the interview, but we did not have that date. There just plain wasn't time. Brock had football practice, and he was senior class president. I had the *Oakleaf*, and in addition I had suddenly become very noticeable. People would stop me in the hall, or phone me at home, asking me to be part of this or that. I found myself on the committee to plan the fall dance. Mike Rafferty, who'd been campaign manager when Brock ran for senior class president last spring, also buttonholed me.

"You're going to be on the Peters team for the Student Council presidency campaign, aren't you, Celia?"

"I don't know if I should," I said reluctantly. "I'm an editor of the school paper."

Mike laughed. "You think Laurie Malone's going to sit the campaign out? Celia, come on! You know you want to, and it won't hurt us to have the press in our corner!" He saw my face and added quickly, "Forget that. I was only joking."

That had been on Thursday. The next day the *Oakleaf* came out with my story, and it dawned on me there was no way anyone could read it and not know I thought Brock

105

Peters was the best thing that ever hit the Oakdale campus. None of the football team was at the movies Friday night, because of curfew, but on Saturday morning, as the team ran out onto the field, Brock winked at me. I was sitting with Michiko and Dorothy in our usual place, the fourth row of bleachers, at the end next to the aisle by the locker rooms.

Zack had flatly refused to spend a morning watching football. It was just as well. We lost, 14–13.

"Some start to the year," Michiko said glumly. "If only Brock hadn't flubbed that pass!"

"It wasn't all his fault!" I flared.

"Sorry, I forgot he's perfect," Michiko said briefly, and changed the subject.

The way she said it made me feel uneasy. Was I being that obvious, I wondered.

Or that blind? The phrase popped up from nowhere, and I pushed it away. I wasn't blind; I knew Brock could be high-handed and arrogant. But that was only because he had so many ideas and talents, so many things he wanted to accomplish. Having to put up with others' slowness made him impatient.

The way he'd been impatient, impulsive

with his pass that morning? Too impatient to make sure he was positioned properly? Or even that passing the ball was the best strategy?

I was so irritated with myself for these disloyal thoughts that I did penance by helping Dad wash the girls that afternoon. Joey helped us both, and I don't know who was the worse mess—Joey, or Susie when she took off through the backyard all lathered with soap.

Joey and I took off after her while Dad, who had more sense, sat back and laughed.

Susie, who thought all this was the greatest fun, kept herself just out of reach. Then we got down by the Peterses' house and Susie cut across the property diagonally, out into the road. Just as a souped-up car came roaring down the road a block away—

I screamed. Joey yelled, "Susie! *Help!*" And a car shot backward out of the Peterses' driveway, straight into the road. The driver slammed on the brakes, barely missing Susie, blocking the whole road. The approaching car's brakes screeched. At the same moment Brock threw open his car door and shouted, "Susie! Come on, girl!" And Susie, like every female, responded to his command.

She jumped in, straight into his lap. A soapy German shepherd squeezed between steering wheel and driver is quite a sight. Her tail hung out, wagging madly.

"Slam the door!" Brock shouted, sliding over to the passenger side. I slammed it quickly. "There's a piece of clothesline in our garage," he called, and Joey ran to get it. We passed it through the partially open window, and Brock tied it firmly through Susie's collar. Then he got out, dragging Susie with him.

By now the other driver was out, too, and saying unprintable things. "Keep your shirt on, buddy," Brock advised. He said to Joey, "Here, take this monster of yours back home and lock her in."

Joey departed, dragging Susie, who looked pleased with herself. I was in my old, too-big jeans, and they were half-soaked. I hung around, anyway. Brock climbed back into his car, pulled it in the driveway, then came toward me, smiling ruefully.

"Not the best day for either of us, is it?"

"What do you mean?"

"Come on, you saw what a jerk I made of myself this morning. Some 'Most Valuable Player Prospect,' wasn't I?" He was quoting my interview.

"You couldn't have known what would go wrong!"

"I could have, if I'd thought. I didn't stop to."

I'd never heard Brock talk like that before. It rocked me; it made him seem far more human. I said impulsively, "It's not your fault if other players are . . . slow on the uptake. Your mind just works faster than most people's. So when you need their cooperation on something, you have to allow for a time gap while they catch up. That's what my dad says."

Brock's face brightened. "Did he really say that? It's darn nice of him."

Actually, Dad had said that in connection with some of his own work at the TV station, but I crossed my fingers and said, "Uh-huh."

"That's a good tip. I'll remember it. And if I don't, you remind me, okay?"

"Okay."

We stood there, half awkwardly. I was slightly breathless and, oddly, he was too. Then we both spoke at once.

"Well, I'd better be getting—"

"Look, Celia—"

We stopped, and Brock said firmly, "This time I'm going to ignore the advice or I'll miss my chance. Last time I asked, you turned me down. Are you going to shoot me down again today, or will you give me some more of the famous Prendergast morale-boosting? I could sure use it."

I asked, very carefully, "What did you have in mind?"

"Dinner tonight," Brock said. "Someplace comfortable and quiet. Soft lights, soft music. Maybe candles stuck in bottles. You tell me what other mistakes I'm making, and what brilliant ideas you have for my Student Council presidency campaign."

My pulse started to hammer. "We don't have to go out to dinner to talk about that," I said faintly.

"We don't," Brock agreed. "But I want to. Right now. Before Collins shows up out of nowhere and carries you off. And we don't have to talk about Student Council, if you don't want to. We don't even have to talk at all."

* * *

We didn't go "right now," because I had a lot of cleaning up to do. But we did go to dinner at a little Italian place Brock knew.

There *were* candles in bottles, and very good pasta, and cannoli. We did talk about his election campaign, but only a little. I had to force myself to act like somebody half in love with another boy. When we went up to the lookout, we hardly saw the magical night glory of the New York skyline. We didn't talk at all. And when Brock kissed me good-night on my own front porch, Zack Collins was the farthest thing from my mind.

NINE

Zack wandered over on Sunday afternoon, bringing Theodore. "Where were you last night? There was a PBS special on turtles on TV. I called to tell you."

"I had dinner out. With Brock."

"Oh?" Zack said. "Congratulations. So I don't suppose you'll want to go for a bike ride with Theodore and me now, will you?"

"Don't be silly. You don't think I'm going to drop you like a hot potato because of one date, do you?" Then I did a double take. "*Theodore* is going for a bike ride?"

"In the basket, stupid. He needs some

fresh air, and I haven't been able to let him out much lately, what with work and school and everything."

"I thought you were going to turn Theodore loose in the pond in your backyard," I commented when Zack and I were pedaling along back roads.

"I was. But his shell still doesn't seem to be healing right. I may have to try to attach a protective shield to it."

"In your spare time?" I asked, grinning.

"Look who's talking." Zack's eyes twinkled. "All I keep hearing around school is 'Celia's doing this' and 'Let's get Celia for that.' And your mom's complaining to mine that she never sees you anymore."

"Parents! They're never satisfied!"

We started pumping up a winding hill. Zack gallantly stayed with me for a while. When he couldn't stand my pace any longer, he shot ahead while I labored after, groaning. He was waiting at the summit, and took pity.

"Want to stop for a while? I brought some sustenance along." He tossed me an apple as I dropped my bike and flopped gratefully underneath a tree. Zack set Theodore in a patch of sun where he craned his neck with interest and snapped at flies. We lay on our backs, chomping apples and comparing notes. Zack told me about Dynachem and the Environmental Club. I told him about my evening with Brock—but not all about it.

Zack looked at me, the corners of his mouth curving up slightly, and I had a disconcerting feeling he was filling in the romantic interlude that I'd omitted. "Looks like 'mission accomplished,' doesn't it?" he said lightly. "You've hooked our hero. Ma's convinced I've become a social butterfly. You want to call our deal off?"

I blinked. "Of course not! One date doesn't mean 'hooked.' Anyway, we're . . . friends. I'd miss you if we stopped hanging around together." I sat up as another uneasy thought struck me. "Unless *you* want to stop."

"Nope. I've kind of gotten used to it, too," Zack said comfortably.

I plopped down again and we were silent for a while. I was thinking, but was not about to say, that Brock's interest was far more likely to continue if he thought I was only semi-available. Anyway, what I'd said to Zack was the absolute truth. I *would* miss him.

* * *

I felt discombobulated when I encountered Brock and Laurie together in school the next day. Not Brock; he flashed me a special smile and said easily, "Can I call you tonight? Celia's going to plot the PR for my Student Council campaign," he added for Laurie's benefit.

"That's great!" Laurie's eyes twinkled. "Just don't forget how busy you're going to be as an *Oakleaf* editor, now that you've made it possible for us to come out every two weeks."

"Oh, Celia's a superwoman." Brock smiled again.

Brock called that night, and we talked about his election strategy. We also talked about going out that weekend. Mindful of my own strategy, I stalled. "Can I let you know? I'm not sure if I'm free."

"Look, you're not Collins's property," Brock said firmly. "Tell him you'll date him Friday and come out Saturday with me. We'll celebrate my winning the football game."

"Pretty sure of yourself, aren't you?" I teased.

"I'll have to do *something* to make up for lousing up last week," Brock said.

When I reported all this to Zack, his comment was succinct. "You're not Peters's property, either. Tell him you already have plans."

So I did. And Brock did not make the winning points at Saturday's game. We lost again, 21–7. The telephone rang that night as I was getting ready for bed.

"Do you feel good and guilty?" Brock's voice inquired in an intimate, half-joking tone. "Where've you been? I've been trying to reach you for two hours."

"I was with Zack." I didn't think it necessary to say our whole family had been over at his house for dinner. "And why should I feel guilty?"

"You wouldn't go out with me tonight," Brock said plaintively. "I had nothing to look forward to except imagining you with Collins. Is it any wonder my game was off?"

In school on Monday people were talking about a jinx on the football team. "So much for your predictions about an outstanding season," Laurie said to me ruefully at the *Oakleaf* meeting.

"Don't blame her. I predicted the same thing," Walter Joyce said with disgust. "What's the matter with those guys? With that lineup, they should be rolling all over the opposition. And they haven't even been up against our stiffest competition yet!"

At the lunch table the comments were more pointed. "Peters was grandstanding," Bruce Hammond said flatly, and Pete Bayer nodded.

"Part grandstanding, and part protecting the gorgeous profile. Last year we had a couple of real hulks to do the heavy hitting, and all Brock had to do was rely on speed and dazzle. He doesn't like to take his lumps with the rest of the line—he likes to be the star."

"There've only been two games. Give the guy a chance," Zack said. "He probably feels awful."

"Not so awful he wasn't laughing up a storm with Laurie at the movies Saturday night," Beth snorted. Then, looking at me, "Oops, sorry."

I waved a sandwich airily. "Don't mind me! I'm playing the field. It's more fun this way."

"Well, Peters had better stop playing the field for popularity and concentrate on his responsibilities, or he's never going to get that Citizenship Award he thinks he has sewn up," Pete said bluntly.

I started. "I thought you two were friends!"

"We are. I just don't subscribe to the theory he's God's gift to Oakdale. But I'm afraid," Pete said soberly, "Brock does believe it."

And he wrote a front-page editorial for the second issue of the *Oakleaf* about how important it was for a broad cross-section of the student body to be involved in all aspects of a school's affairs. It urged everyone to be active, run for offices, serve on committees, rather than surrender leadership automatically to a small clique.

It didn't mention Brock by name. That, I would have noticed. As it was, the paper came out during lunchtime Friday, and I'm ashamed to say all I did was glance at it quickly to be sure nothing had gone wrong with the pages for which I was responsible. As soon as art class was over, I hurried home. We were heading to Vermont to visit my grandparents for the weekend, and Mother had written Joey and me notes so we could leave school early.

My grandparents' place was beautiful at this time of year. Trees up the mountains were beginning to turn, but the air was warm, the dogs could run loose to their hearts' content, and I had nothing to do but bask in my grandparents' admiration over how grown-up I'd become.

"Oh, yes, life is getting very interesting," Mother agreed with a mock sigh.

I did wonder once, Saturday morning, how our football game was going. But other than that I didn't really think about Oakdale, or the people in it, at all. It was really restful.

We got home after midnight on Sunday, far too late for anyone who might have been trying to phone me to call. Probably because of the late return, we all overslept on Monday morning. By the time I got to school, I'd missed homeroom entirely. A special assembly was in progress. Of course, I thought, hurrying to the auditorium. Today was the day campaigns for Student Council offices officially began, with the circulation of nominating petitions. Candidates had three days to seek the required number of signatures, then a week and a half for campaigning before elections took place on a Friday. Mr. McPhail always made a speech this opening day, pleading that the school's regular business of education go on uninterrupted while the carnival atmosphere prevailed.

As I opened an auditorium door a crack and skinned through, I wished that Brock and I had had a chance to talk before school. No posters for a candidate could be hung until that candidate's petition had been filed, and it wasn't considered sporting to make the posters ahead of time, either. But Brock would have no difficulty getting his signatures. If I knew Mike Rafferty, he probably had the petition tucked in his notebook right now and would start circulating it the minute Mr. McPhail gave the word. So it would be smart to have the posters and other campaign gimmicks all planned ahead and ready to roll. I'd already made a list of slogans to suggest.

I slid into a seat at the end of a back row. Mr. McPhail was talking and holding up Friday's issue of the *Oakleaf.*

". . . must congratulate the editors and staff of this year's *Oakleaf,* and their faculty adviser, on the vital new direction they've given to the paper."

Laurie will be happy, I thought, pleased. Then the rest of what Mr. McPhail was saying started sinking in.

". . . fine editorial that I understand was written by Pete Bayer, the news editor."

Applause, and muffled laughter, as Pete stood up and clasped his hands above his head. "I could not agree more with his plea for more widespread student involvement, not just in council elections but in all school affairs. Not, as we've usually had these past few years, the government and activities of many students in the hands of just a few."

There was another muted burst of applause. But at the same time, something in the atmosphere of the room was changing. Mr. McPhail straightened. "Actually, this editorial turns out to be part of what science teachers refer to as a 'simultaneous phenomena.' It dovetails exactly with a ruling the high school's administrative board made last week. In the interests of broadening student leadership, as well as making sure no one or two students end up with more burdens than can successfully be carried, the board has ruled that henceforth no student may fill both an elected class office and an elected Student Council office at the same time."

Uproar.

"*Therefore,*" the principal overrode the din firmly, "no nominating petitions will be accepted for any student currently serving as president, vice president, secretary, or treasurer of his or her class. Ladies and gentlemen, the campaigns for Student Council officers are now open, and may the best candidates win!"

The lights in the auditorium snapped on. The bells sounded. The student body surged out of rows into the aisles. The noise was terrific, and for once no teacher tried to stop it.

May the best candidate win. Brock Peters was the best choice, and the whole school knew it. His election—though Brock himself had been careful not to act that way—was a foregone conclusion; it had been for years. But Brock was already president of the senior class.

Brock could not run for Student Council president.

TEN

I went through my morning classes on automatic pilot. My brain wasn't functioning.

In the cafeteria at lunchtime, everyone was buzzing. Petitions were circulating. At our usual table my lunch crowd was talking about the election bombshell a mile a minute. Not Zack, though. He took a look at me, deliberately draped his arm across the back of my chair, and sat back to take it all in.

"It was your editorial," Dorothy told Pete. Pete shrugged.

"I can't take the credit. I didn't know about the board meeting, and the board didn't see what I'd written. I just said something I thought needed to be said."

"It was time somebody said it," Bruce agreed.

"It wasn't fair, though, that the ruling came the same day that petitions started," Michiko put in, her eyes on me. "The board should have decided last June, before class elections were held, so everybody knew the same person couldn't be elected twice. Brock would have made a good council president."

"Sure, but so would some other kids, and now they'll have half a chance," Pete said equably. "Peters can concentrate on being a good class president. Or on his football, for a change."

"Where is Peters, anyway?" It was Zack who asked, not me, although I was wondering the same thing.

"He's not here. I guess he couldn't take it and left." Beth's voice was uncharacteristically biting.

Laurie Malone was passing our table, and she heard. She stopped. "Brock has a doctor's appointment," she said, her tone carefully even. "Because of what happened to his shoulder on Saturday."

"What did happen at the game on Saturday?" I made myself ask casually when she had gone.

Everyone looked at me. "Didn't you hear?" Pete said. "We lost—again. And Brock tore a ligament in his shoulder."

Bad as that was, I was glad Brock had a legitimate excuse for leaving. The mood in the cafeteria . . . I could not put my finger on the right adjective, but it was not complimentary. Oakdale High School almost seemed glad to see its hero cut down to size.

In art class the talk turned to who was now likely to become council president, and who was best among the candidates for the other offices. "Who are you going to vote for, Celia?" Scott Levine, *Oakleaf*'s photo editor, asked.

"Don't know yet," I answered lightly.

"Why don't you run for something?"

I did a double take.

"Why don't you?" Roberta Wills asked.

"I'm an underclassman. Anyway, I'm not the type."

"Sure you are," Laurie put in, to my surprise. "The seniors would vote for you— I'm sure of it. If you don't want to run for anything this time, at least think about running for vice-president next year."

"But the vice presidency's like a trial run for the presidency in your senior year," I sputtered.

"So?" Laurie retorted, smiling. "Everyone knows you're a hard worker and you're concerned about the school. And you've already proved you're a real leader, with the *Oakleaf*. You're features editor, not news, so there isn't really a conflict of interest. Even if you wound up council president and editor in chief at the same time, you could always disqualify yourself from working on certain stories."

"I have enough to do without being an officer," I murmured, feeling dazed. But the very suggestion, and the support it had received, were accolades to treasure in my heart.

Zack had to work at Dynachem that afternoon. I avoided Michiko and walked home from school alone. When I walked past the Peterses' house, the car wasn't there, and there was no sign of Brock. I wondered how badly his shoulder had been hurt. And that wasn't all I wondered.

I went home, and fought the temptation to telephone him. At dinner, as lightly as possible, I told my family what had taken place. My parents, to my irritation, agreed with Mr. McPhail. "It's never good for any organization to always be steered by the same small group," Dad said.

"Not to mention that everything's always come easily to Brock. It won't hurt him to have to share the spotlight," Mother added.

I stared at them. "I thought you liked Brock!"

"That's beside the point." Mother looked me squarely in the eyes. "Tell the truth, Celia. Don't you appreciate being an editor of the *Oakleaf* more because you worked all last year to earn it? People to whom honors and recognition come easily usually start expecting them as a matter of course. The rude awakening can be devastating if they're not equipped to handle disappointment."

"It often doesn't happen till they're out of school and in the real world," Dad said. "Then you see yesterday's heroes still reliving the triumphs of their school careers. They've never had to work hard for anything before, or they've never knocked themselves out and found that still was not enough. It can be pretty sad."

I pushed back my chair. "You're not being fair! Brock does work hard. And he inspires others to work hard with him!" I fished for words. "Look at me—I'd never be doing all the things I'm taking on this year, if I hadn't learned how from Brock!"

"I thought Zack was entitled to the credit for that," Mother murmured dryly.

"Oh, you just don't understand!"

I wasn't altogether sure I did myself, and that made me all the madder.

I stormed upstairs on a full head of steam, and I was so worked up I did something I'd never thought I could. I picked up the phone and called Pete Bayer.

"Hi, Celia," he said cheerfully when he heard my voice. "What's up? You want to do some brainstorming? We'll have to take a whole different tack on our next issue, as a result of the board's decision. Want to do some features to complement my front-page lead?"

"Don't you 'Hi, Celia' me," I retorted. "And don't talk to me about dovetailing our departments. That was some dirty trick you pulled with your editorial!"

"Hey, wait a minute! I didn't know what action the board was planning! I was merely expressing my own opinions, and I stand by them. And I didn't have to consult you before I expressed them," Pete pointed out.

"Would you want to have to get my okay on what you put in your feature pages? I did check, with Laurie, because she's editor in chief, and she agreed."

"*Laurie* okayed the story?"

"She had to, didn't she," Pete asked, "since it was an editorial? Sure she okayed it. Why wouldn't she? Sixteen kids a year are class officers, and lots of times they've been council officers as well. All I said was, spread the power and the glory around a little."

"There's also work involved," I said acidly.

"Don't I know it. Why do you think I'm graciously declining to run? Handling too many jobs at once can be a pain in the you-know-what."

"Brock could have handled it," I said stubbornly. "You let your personal feelings about him interfere with your journalistic objectivity, and got the rules changed in the middle of the game. And that's not fair!"

I was ignoring the question of how an editorial published on a Friday could have influenced an administrative decision earlier that week. Of course, some faculty members would have seen it—Mr. Oliver, Mr. Fontanazza, the computer teacher. Had they leaked to McPhail?

Pete didn't pick that up. He went straight for the jugular. "*What* journalistic objectivity? Nowhere in the whole piece was Brock's name mentioned, so why are you jumping to the conclusion it was a personal attack on Brock? Next year *you* may have to decide between being class officer or a Student Council officer. If Zack Collins had moved here a year ago, he might be in Brock's spot now."

I actually said, "Huh?"

"He might have been a senior class officer, you dope," Pete said patiently. "He got elected president of the Environmental Club Friday afternoon, didn't he? And incidentally, Celia, if you're going to turn into a mother hen about the men in your life, you might consider that what's bad for one of them could be good for the other."

"What are you talking about?"

"Zack's pals in the Environmental Club want him to run for council president. Didn't you know?"

Blessedly, there was a beep on the phone, thanks to the call-waiting feature that Dad had recently had installed in case there was an emergency at the TV station. "There's another call," I mumbled hastily. "I'd better hang up."

I did so, my head spinning. The phone rang again and I picked it up. Please don't let it be Zack, I prayed. Not till I get my act together. Because Zack, knowing kids wanted him to run for office, had nonetheless sat there at lunch and never said a word because he knew how badly I'd wanted Brock to win.

It wasn't Zack on the phone. Brock's voice, very subdued, said, "Celia?"

"Brock! How's your arm?"

"I'll live," Brock said wryly. "I haven't yet decided whether that's an advantage or a disadvantage. Look, are you doing anything right now?"

I wet my lips. "What did you have in mind?"

"Feel like lending me a listening ear? And maybe a sympathetic shoulder? I have a lot of thinking to do."

"Sure," I said, careful to sound casual. Acting as if I felt sorry for him would be fatal. "But not on the phone. You want to come over? We could sit out on the porch."

"I don't think I can sit still," Brock said. "You feel like walking to the lookout?"

So that's what we did. I waited for him on the porch, so he didn't have to get involved with my family, and when I saw his shape moving in the darkness across the lawn, I ran to meet him. His right arm was done up in a sling, but he took my right hand with his left one and we walked in silence up to the lookout. We sat down on top of the stone wall that looked out across the county to New York City. I glanced at Brock, and Brock stared down and away.

"How is your arm, really?" I asked.

"Hurts like hell, if you must know. I tore a couple of ligaments, so I won't be playing football for a few weeks. Maybe not for the rest of the season." Brock was silent for a minute. "Maybe that's good luck for the team."

"Don't talk like that."

"Why not? It's the truth, isn't it?" Brock picked a pebble off the wall and flung it out into the darkness. "I've been facing up to a few unpleasant truths all day. I'm not going to be the shining light of this year's graduating class, after all. I was doing lousy at football, anyway. I'm not sure why. Now I can't be Student Council president. Are you still willing to be seen with me if I'm no longer 'Most Likely to Succeed'?"

"What do you think I am?" I asked

indignantly. "You don't honestly think I went out with you only because you were a football star?"

"Lots of girls would," Brock said bluntly. "Sorry if I sound cynical, but I've known that ever since I was in seventh grade. And people think only women know what it's like to be regarded as a piece of meat!"

"Brock, stop it!"

"The worst of it," Brock said after a minute, in a different voice, "is knowing I'm letting my old man down. It matters a lot to him, me being a letterman and leader and all that. It's a family tradition. You're a winner or you're nothing."

"You don't really believe that."

Brock went on as if he hadn't heard. "And the scholarships. That's the big thing. I get by, but I'm not a brain. I really need an athletic scholarship, and the Citizenship Award and scholarship, to get into a good college." He looked at his arm. "I'm getting a deferment of this marking period's writing assignments for a few weeks, so I guess I should be grateful for small mercies."

"*Will you listen to me?*" I took a deep breath. "No! Listen to yourself! That's not the Brock Peters who would have gotten elected council president talking; that's a quitter." Brock's head snapped around, eyes blazing, and I pressed my advantage. "Like my dad was saying, things always mean more when they come harder. They'll mean more to the others who are watching, too. So you miss the football season and being president of Student Council. You still play baseball, don't you? You're still the president of the senior class."

"I didn't want to concentrate just on class activities," Brock said. "If I'd known I'd have to choose between jobs, I'd have chosen council. Some years the Student Council can really make a difference. Not just in school, but in the community. Like you guys mean to do with the *Oakleaf*."

"Since when is the council the only way to do that? Work on the *Oakleaf*." I rushed on as he laughed and shook his head. "Or get active in some other group." I was remembering Zack and the Environmental Club. "You're in Civics Club, aren't you? They haven't held elections yet. Run for president of that! Heck, you're eighteen; run for the Board of Education! High school students in other towns have been elected."

Brock was looking at me with respect. Suddenly, his eyes kindled, and he wrapped his good arm around me and pulled me close. "Celia, you're the best thing that's happened to me this fall. You never give up, do you?"

"Not when I believe in people," I said.

"Then I'm very glad that you believe in me. I won't let *you* down, I promise." He released me slightly, then bent forward and kissed me, very gently, on the lips.

ELEVEN

Zack didn't run for Student Council president. "What for?" he asked when I told him I'd heard about the suggestion. "I just want to look involved enough in school to keep Ma off my back. I'm not going to give it my body and soul, even if it would be good for my image. That's not how I get my jollies."

"Herbert Zachary Collins," I sputtered, "you're the limit! I wasn't suggesting you go for an office because of image. I was suggesting it because it's important and worthwhile, and it might be fun!" I shot him a sideways look. "You didn't mind getting elected president of the Environmental Club. And you didn't even tell me about it."

Zack shrugged. "I didn't think you'd think it was any big deal. You told me the club was pretty small potatoes."

"But I suppose it's fun."

"Yup. It is." He gave me a wicked glance. "Why don't you try it? Are you telling me you don't get a charge out of wading in the muck rescuing the native fauna?"

Since at that moment Theodore was lying in my lap while I fed him dehydrated flies, that was a loaded question. "This one fauna is enough for me," I answered sweetly. "Why don't you join me on the *Oakleaf*? You could write crusading pieces about saving the environment in idyllic Oakdale."

Zack, who was polluting the environment by tossing homemade chemical pellets in our living-room fire, causing the flames to turn green and purple, rolled over on his back and grinned. "What about you? You going to file for office before the deadline?"

So he'd heard about Laurie's suggestion. I wondered where. "Not me. That's not how I get my jollies, either."

"The power of the press is greater than

the power of the throne?" Zack asked innocently. "Or are you addicted to being the power behind the throne? Better watch it, kid, you're reverting."

I threw a magazine at him. Zack threw it back, and followed that with a couple of pine cones. Theodore slid off my lap and took refuge under the couch, and Susie and Missy bounded in to join the fray. The result was a ruckus, and no more embarrassing talk about elections. It was, all in all, a rather satisfactory Saturday night.

All through autumn, that was the pattern of my days, and of my dates. Celia and Zack; Celia and Brock. We were becoming a notable school triangle, or so I learned from Michiko, who kept me up-to-date. Nobody, apparently, could figure it out.

Brock was also still dating Laurie, and, as always, he had groupies following him around. Some of them followed him into Civics Club, and they certainly helped get him elected its president. Zack wasn't dating anyone but me, at least as far as I knew. Both mothers, his and mine, had heart-to-hearts with me. Mine was relieved I wasn't getting too serious with either boy. Aunt Lenore was concerned that Zack might be hurt. It was not the kind of autumn I'd ever had before.

Oh, yes, Mike Rafferty wound up Student Council president. Brock was his campaign manager, for a change. That caused quite a stir in school, and I was happy to see it earned Brock much respect. So much for the hints he was only out for number one!

"I've been thinking about what you said about running for the Board of Education," Brock told me when we were out celebrating Mike's election. "Not this November. It's too late to start, and I don't know enough about what's involved. But I'd like to brainstorm with you about positioning myself for next year."

"What about college?"

"I've been talking to my dad. I may apply to Rutgers. I could commute to classes. I'd still be around Oakdale for meetings." He flashed his celebrated crooked grin. "Heck, this is still the face that launched a thousand footballs, isn't it? Not to mention school elections, and selling candy and light bulbs and greeting cards for Little League! Like they say, if you've got it, flaunt it. It's time I used the old charm for something worthwhile, don't you think?"

I glowed at him.

As the October days passed, the hillsides did their own flaunting in their autumn colors, and our football team continued to lose. Somehow, people were forgetting Brock's less-than-spectacular record in the early games and were consoling themselves with, "Oh, well, what could we expect with Peters sidelined?"

Time was sliding past me at a steadily accelerating speed. It was measured out by those every-other-week *Oakleaf* deadlines. I was spending an awful lot of out-of-school time in Room 213, and my parents began making noises about my forgetting chores around the house. But they weren't really sore. Actually, I think my mother was overjoyed. She was finally seeing me repeat her old school pattern.

"Just be glad I'm not trying to hold down a job, too, the way Zack is," I told her when she began to fret that I wasn't getting enough sleep.

"Don't tell me about that," Mother said ruefully. "I had lunch with Lenore. Zack's getting so psyched up by what he's seeing at Dynachem that he's making noises about entering Columbia or New York University this spring, instead of waiting till after graduation, and trying to do his under-graduate work in just two years!"

"I'll talk to him, I'll talk to him," I promised.

I got, or made, a chance that Saturday. It was a glowing, golden day, and I phoned Zack early, before he had a chance to take off for parts unknown. "You don't have to work today, do you? Feel like packing up one of those organic picnics of yours and biking in the hills?"

"You're not going to the football game?" Zack inquired, mock-horrified. "Tired of seeing the team lose, or is it too boring with your hero sidelined?"

"You shut up," I said severely. Actually, he'd hit the nail right on the head. But we didn't talk about Brock, or about school affairs. We pedaled single file, the lunch in Zack's basket and Theodore, who weighed less than the food, in mine. It felt good to be outdoors, to be aimless, to not be thinking about deadlines hanging over me.

It wasn't till we were lying on our backs, gazing up at the sun and the red-gold glory of the trees while Theodore slumbered on my middle, that I remembered what I'd come for.

"What's all this about starting college in January? You're not thinking about skipping the rest of senior year?"

"Heck, no. I should be able to handle both. Butter up McPhail to let me cram all my solid subjects into morning slots, then take the train to the city for college courses in the afternoon." Zack rolled over on his side to face me, looking enthusiastic. "I've been talking to one of the guys in the labs at Dynachem. He did that, and it worked fine. He earned his B.S. in two and a half years, by going summers, and had everything but his doctoral dissertation done by the time his high school classmates were finishing up their bachelor's degrees. Dynachem snapped him up, they were so impressed!"

"And he's been a Dynachem clone ever since."

"Sure, why not?" Zack was puzzled. "Sure, the company has a cookie-cutter white-collar image. You're the one who told me uniforms are important, remember? But that's all it is, a uniform. It's really a fun place to work."

Knowing Zack's definition of fun was not the same as mine, I didn't bother to argue with him.

"Anyway," Zack said happily, "this Bob Herskovitz thinks there may be a real future for me at Dynachem. He'd like to see me stay and go up the ladder with him."

"Is that what you really want?" I asked, frowning. "What happened to marine biology? Going off on expeditions like Cousteau, just you and your diving suit and the water creatures?"

Zack tickled Theodore's nose with a blade of grass. Theodore woke up, snapped at it halfheartedly, and went back to sleep. "That's the beauty of it," Zack said. "Nothing's been definitely announced yet. But it's ninety percent sure that within the next five years Dynachem's going to be entering marine biology in a big way. The sea as the source of nutrients and pharmaceuticals, you know. It's the last great frontier, now that we've reached the moon!"

Zack was in one of his exultant, boyish moods, and my heart melted. "And you want in on it?"

"Darn right I do! If I keep on at Dynachem part-time, and have my graduate degrees by then, I'll have both big feet in the door! And I wouldn't be tied to head-quarters either, Bob says. By then Dynachem may be chartering one of Columbia's research ships. And get this, Celia. The Dynachem complex here will be world headquarters for the whole marine-based products operation! They have the perfect location for it, near the Hudson River harbors and all that land!"

I sat up, dislodging Theodore. "I haven't heard about anything like that."

"It isn't public yet. But Dynachem's at the halfway point in a ten-year plan." A worried look crossed Zack's face. "I probably shouldn't have shot my mouth off like this. Bob said the marine products expansion is still top secret. Something to do with financing and competition. But the first step in the expansion of the Oakdale plant will soon be common knowledge. Dynachem's going to file for zoning board approval next week."

I never did get around to giving Zack that speech about slowing down.

TWELVE

━━━◆━━━

We didn't get back home till late afternoon, and the first thing that greeted me was Joey, making loud kissing noises and announcing, "Superjock's been calling you all afternoon!"

I hurried into the house, and Mother said, "He's coming to pick you up at seven-thirty. Nice of him to assume your answer's yes."

"Don't start."

"I wasn't planning to," Mother said grandly. "I was merely reporting a fact."

I phoned Brock, and he sounded subdued. The football team had lost again. He wanted to take me out to dinner but didn't have enough cash, so would going for a ride and ending up for ice cream somewhere be okay?

"That's fine," I said. "Or we could go Dutch. If you don't mind my asking, how come you're so strapped?"

"Thanks for the offer, but let me hang on to my chauvinist pride a little longer." Brock groaned. "I got laid off. That idiot I work for bawled me out for coming in five minutes late again. Well, maybe ten minutes, but I haven't done it all that often. And selling T-shirts at the game for the Civics Club war fund is more important than flipping hamburgers, anyway."

"Brock, you didn't tell him that!"

"Sure I did," Brock admitted ruefully. "Don't worry. I'll hustle another job somewhere soon. Tonight I'd rather just forget the whole thing!"

So I dressed carefully, in cinnamon-colored slacks and bulky sweater, and sprayed perfume liberally. We rode up through the hills, and I didn't say I'd been there that day already. We wound up buying pint containers of ice cream, and parking by the reservoir, and snuggling in the backseat to eat and smooch.

And talk. More and more Brock was talking to me in a way I sensed he never had with a girl before. He let down his guard with me. Tonight he was talking about the frustrations of still being in high school, and wanting to do things, things that mattered, and not being able to. "Ironic, isn't it? I thought my senior year was going to be the absolute pinnacle, and now that I'm here, I catch myself thinking, 'Is this all there is?'"

Of course, he'd expected to be playing football. And running the school, through Student Council. And earning money. I didn't say that. I said instead, "You'll find a job. Why don't you try at Dynachem?"

"Where Collins works? No, thanks, I'm not the lab mole type. Anyway, they're not hiring. They even had to lay people off last spring."

"They'll be hiring again soon." I stopped abruptly. Brock straightened, his eyes alert.

"Don't stop. You were just about to say something."

"I suppose it won't hurt. Dynachem's going to go to the zoning board next week, anyway. They're planning a major expansion of their Oakdale facilities, and that would mean more jobs, wouldn't it?" It seemed safe to say that much.

"It sure would! You don't know the half of it." He was suddenly the old Brock again, dynamic and elated. "Celia, I've been getting the Civics Club working on a survey of the hidden unemployment here in Oakdale. You'd be surprised how many families, families like ours, are on unemployment. They're not used to it, they're ashamed, they keep it quiet. But if Dynachem's going to expand—"

He shifted position. I could almost hear his mind racing. "There's a ripple effect. It won't mean just jobs at Dynachem, but for other businesses that service it. Real estate values will go up. And tax money! Maybe the school will finally be able to enlarge the gym and cafeteria!" He opened the car door. "Come on, let's go!"

"Where?"

"Back to your house, and get on the phone. Here's a real project for Civics Club, and for the *Oakleaf*! Have you forgotten what it's like to try to get zoning variances through in Oakdale?"

"Of course not! There're always a few people who want to keep the town like it was in the good old days."

"Exactly. And sometimes they've made enough noise to throw roadblocks in the way of progress for years. Oakdale needs more jobs, and more tax money, *now.* Maybe we can help get that message across to people!"

We ended up with an unofficial joint meeting of the *Oakleaf* staff, the Civics Club officers, and Student Council president Mike Rafferty around the table in our dining room. I sneaked upstairs to telephone Zack and confess my sins.

"I don't think you've done any harm," he agreed. "Just keep quiet about the marine project, understand? I'll tell Bob tomorrow. If the leak is anybody's fault, it's mine. But Peters's idea just might be a very good one."

* * *

On Wednesday evening the zoning board received Dynachem's expansion request for consideration. Since debate on a proposed subdivision was also on the agenda, the meeting had a large attendance. It did *not* include members of the Oakdale High School student body, at Dad's insistence. "You'd only be advertising you had advance knowledge, and that would do more harm than good." But he went, and he brought back a report that the session had been heated.

"Dynachem's in for a struggle. A couple of old hands on the board remember when the original Dynachem building was approved, and how the company promised it would remain regional headquarters only."

On Thursday, as predicted, the story broke on the front page of *The Record*. There was also an editorial, saluting the promise of future jobs but warning about ecological dangers and overload on the town's facilities. By coincidence, the lead story in the local news section was on the Board of Education's umpteenth proposal for a school bond issue to enlarge the high school. And there were letters to the editor from people who had been at the zoning meeting and who were reacting strongly, both pro and con.

"Here we go!" Brock said happily when he read all this.

On Friday the *Oakleaf*, with my feature story on Dynachem, appeared—the result of a lot of last-minute hustle. The paper hit the cafeteria at the end of the first lunch period. It went home from school with students and with teachers, and it was, as always, delivered to the town library and town officials as a courtesy. When my father came home from work that night, he was grinning.

"I had three phone calls asking if you were my daughter. The station news staff want to know if they can interview you, as a human interest story showing the good side of teenagers, and all that."

"It wasn't just me. It was all of us," I protested, pleased. "Especially Brock!"

It wasn't only the public television station that was interested in teens-as-good-citizens. *The Record* sent a reporter and photographer to school to interview the *Oakleaf* staff, the Civics Club, and the Student Council. And Zack, as student-scientist-who-works-for-Dynachem. Zack had to get permission from Dynachem for the interview, and he was very cautious. But his enthusiasm showed through.

The story ran in *The Record* Tuesday night, and focused primarily on Brock, and Zack, and me, and Laurie. Michiko's lips twitched when she saw that. "Good thing they left your complicated love lives out of it," she murmured. I turned scarlet. But the newspaper story did one thing. It linked Brock and Zack, that odd couple, in the public eye as allies.

It did something else, too. Dad's station didn't get the scoop on us teen angels, after all. CBS sent a reporter and camera crew to interview Brock and me, in front of the Elephant's stone living-room fireplace. Zack was interviewed, too, but his part of the tape ended up on the cutting-room floor—possibly, as Dad suggested, because the editor felt it would be a plug for Dynachem. Theodore made it on, though, settled comfortably in my lap.

"Nothing like animals to tug the heartstrings," Dad chuckled.

It felt funny seeing myself on television. I felt uncomfortable about Zack not being there, too. But Zack, who along with Aunt Lenore was watching in our living room, didn't mind.

"I'd rather be one of the guys in the white coats in the back room. Let Celia have the glory."

"And Brock Peters," Aunt Lenore said. There was an odd note in her voice.

I looked up startled. Her face was ambiguous. But Zack and my mother were both nodding.

"Celia definitely came over the best in the interview," Zack said. "I know Peters is sincere about this whole business, but he didn't sound it. Can't somebody stop him from sounding like a game show host?"

THIRTEEN

The proposed Dynachem expansion came up
right before local elections and made those
elections a very hot issue. The planning board
would have to say yes or no to Dynachem's
plans, and the planning board members were
appointed by Oakdale's elected town council.
Several of the council members' terms
expired this year, so who got elected to the
council could make a lot of difference to the
Dynachem expansion. And Dynachem's
expansion could make a big difference when
the school budget—not to mention Board of
Education candidates, and perhaps a bond

issue for school expansion—came up for a vote next spring.

Needless to say, Oakdale High School students getting involved in community issues, via the school newspaper and school clubs, was very hot stuff. It had never happened before. It wouldn't have happened now if Mr. Oliver weren't the *Oakleaf*'s new faculty adviser. Or for that matter, if it weren't for Brock and Zack, and Laurie's wanting the *Oakleaf* to become more than just a teen gossip sheet.

A lot of people liked things better the old way, and said so in letters to the editors of all the area newspapers. The pros and cons of the Dynachem expansion—and how it would affect Oakdale's life and finances—became big issues in the town council candidates' campaigns.

"I never knew small-town politics could be such a big deal!" I said.

"You never paid any attention to local elections before," Mom retorted. "Anyway, a major chemical company enlarging its operations is not a small issue. Or even a local one. It could affect the environment of the whole metropolitan area."

You don't know the half of it, I thought,

remembering what Zack had confided about the future marine biology division.

Brock was a wonder. Having realized what a boon the Dynachem expansion could be to Oakdale and how teens could help make it happen, he didn't waste a moment. The day after the issue broke in the news, the Civics Club swung into action. School clubs weren't allowed to take political stands, but there was no reason they couldn't "educate the public" about the need for school expansion. And there was no reason any of us, strictly as individuals, couldn't point out that more Dynachem equaled more jobs equaled more money into the town coffers, directly or indirectly. Not that everybody agreed with us. Far from it.

"One of Dad's higher-ups came up to him at a meeting today," Brock reported disgustedly in one of his now nightly phone calls. "He wanted to let him know, confidentially, that he'd better rein me in, and that it wasn't a good idea for me to tread on toes."

"How did that go over?" I asked.

Brock laughed. "It would have been a lot worse if one of their biggest clients hadn't strolled up at that moment. He congratulated

Dad on my civic conscience, and asked if I could speak to a business group he's in!"

"That's wonderful!"

"It gives me an idea," Brock said. "Why couldn't we put together a presentation, and try to present it at as many places as possible before Election Day? Why don't you get some committees working? I wouldn't have time to do all the speaking myself, of course, but some of the other kids could do it, couldn't they?"

I spent the rest of the evening brainstorming and making phone calls.

"I thought you weren't a member of that Civics Club," Michiko commented when I told her all this as we walked to school the next morning.

"I guess I've become a member by default. Anyway, this isn't Civics Club, not officially. What about you? You can do something in the presentations, can't you?"

"I'm a musician, not a public speaker," Michiko said. "Besides, I haven't made up my mind yet whether having a bigger chemical company in town is a good idea. I don't know enough about it yet. And how are you going to squeeze all this lobbying in before Election Day?

Michiko was right. I came back to reality with a dull thud. Here I already had a committee making calls to every official and unofficial group in town, not to mention the campaign managers of the candidates, seeking permission to present our spiel. Where was that spiel going to come from?

I'd opened Pandora's box when I wrote that feature for the *Oakleaf*, I thought ruefully. But that had been easy. All I'd had to do was interview Zack and get Scott Levine to take some pictures. Writing an article was easy compared to organizing a presentation. And for that matter, a picture was worth a thousand words—

A picture was worth a thousand words! I sat up straight. Nobody—except Brock, of course— was wild about getting up in front of audiences and making speeches. But how about talking informally, the way we'd done with that reporter from *The Record?* Or having Scott shoot our pictures, the way he often fooled around before and after school with his video camera or the school's videotape equipment?

Why couldn't we make a video of conditions at school, the good and the bad, and also of Dynachem being a good citizen and neighbor?

I was so excited I reached immediately for the telephone. I had the good sense to call Scott first, since it was Scott's photographic talents on which the whole enterprise depended. Fortunately, Scott was all for it.

Then I called the Collinses' house, but got no answer. Aunt Lenore must be working late, and Zack was probably at Dynachem. It dawned on me all at once that I was taking a lot on myself plunking Zack, a Dynachem employee, in the middle of a very noticeable political action campaign focusing on Dynachem.

This was a matter that called for face-to-face negotiation.

I ran downstairs, calling out that I'd be back soon. It was cold out, and very dark. Halloween was only a few days away. Maybe we could get a gang from the high school to go out trick-or-treating—with informative flyers on the high school, how great it was, how much it needed enlarged facilities.

I parked myself on the Collinses' front steps and waited for Zack to come home. Aunt Lenore got there first, and looked at me in surprise. "What's the matter, your folks throw you out?" she asked dryly.

"I have to talk to Zack."

"Come on in. He should be home sometime in the next hour, if he doesn't forget he has a home. Turning him loose at Dynachem is just like when I gave him his first chemistry set. He loses all track of time." Aunt Lenore's eyes twinkled. "You'd better eat dinner with me while we're waiting. I brought home plenty of Chinese takeout."

She phoned to break that information to my mother, and we sat around the pretty, country kitchen eating spicy beef with orange sauce and talking girl talk. Neither of us had had much time for that lately, and it was fun. Then Zack came home and took possession of the remaining food. "What have you women been gossiping about behind my back?" he inquired.

"It's called networking," Aunt Lenore retorted in her best executive tone. I blushed, of course. Zack looked at me shrewdly.

"Was it about my personal life, or yours, or your latest attack of civic conscience?"

"You heard about that?" I asked lamely.

Zack grinned. "I ran into Scott Levine on my way home. You want my help, you got it. I have a few ideas. I also have a star for your production." He went to the corner and scooped something up from a basket on the floor.

I stared. *"Theodore?"*

"Why not? Everyone's a sucker for animals. Theodore has personality. You can photograph him in his natural habitat at the Dynachem stream. You can even cart him around to make personal appearances. He's a natural PR gimmick," Zack said smugly, offering Theodore a piece of bean sprout.

"I thought he was going back to his natural habitat before the cold weather," Aunt Lenore murmured. Zack shrugged that off with one more excuse about how Theodore's shell hadn't fully mended. Behind Zack's back, Aunt Lenore's eyes met mine, twinkling.

We now had a plan of action, a format, subject matter—and a star.

* * *

Laurie and I wrote the script for our little opus, with assistance from other *Oakleaf* trained school writers. Mr. Oliver critiqued it unofficially, and Mr. Fontanazza, also unofficially, scaled our grandiose plans down to manageable size. Somehow or other, the film was made before our first booking came up the night before Halloween.

After the presentation everyone involved, including Theodore, returned to the Elephant through a night filled with weird noises, illegal firecrackers, and toilet paper-streamered trees. Brock was in his mountain-toppling mood.

"Here's to Oakdale and the high school gearing up for the twenty-first century, *at last!*"

"How about to Celia's efforts on that behalf?" Zack inquired in a very even tone.

My head came up sharply, to intercept a meeting of eyes that jolted me. I had never seen easygoing Zack with that look in his eyes before.

"Oh, everybody worked hard," I said hurriedly.

"Not as hard as you did. It's all been your idea, from start to finish," Zack said deliberately.

Brock gave me a light squeeze and laughed easily. "Sure, she's worked hard. Celia's a big girl—she doesn't need you running guard for her. She's not your property, after all."

"And she's not your slave."

I wasn't sure I heard that; it was said very low. Fortunately, at that moment Laurie raised her glass of cider. "Here's to Theodore! He was our real star tonight!"

Of course, everyone had fallen in love with Theodore.

During the week that followed, Theodore treated his growing celebrity with bland indifference. He was the only one who did. He was the hit of the junior-senior high school Halloween party, held in the blind hope of eliminating the usual egg throwing, chalk scrawling, et cetera. He went to the Lions Club, the Rotary Club, the Chamber of Commerce, the Women's Club, several business and professional organizations, and assorted PTAs. A couple of council candidates were photographed with him, to the annoyance of other candidates who hadn't thought of it.

By the time Election Day rolled around, Theodore was more of a public figure than some of the local candidates, and Brock and Zack were not far behind.

"And you, too," Michiko said pointedly as we gloated over the photograph of Theodore & Co. that had made the front page of *The Record.*

"I only hope I've done enough," I replied.

If I had, it was just barely. The elections resulted in the council being split almost evenly between the pro-industrial expansionists and the traditionalists. The planning board declared that any decision on Dynachem's application for expansion would be postponed till after the first of the year, and would not be made until after public hearings.

FOURTEEN

———◆———

Winter was beginning. Sometimes it comes late in New Jersey, and sometimes early. This was one of the early years. Three days of raw, uninterrupted rain and wind knocked the last leaves off the trees. Dad started building fires in our fireplace more frequently. In school the student body, having given up any hopes of a winning football season, began looking forward to Christmas vacation and the annual New Year's Eve dance. This was an Oakdale tradition, not a prom but a fund-raising formal held by the senior class to underwrite graduation festivities.

"Who are you going to go with?" Michiko asked me.

"It's too soon to say. Zack, probably. I'm sure Brock will ask Laurie." Actually, I wasn't sure of any such thing. I was just saving face in case that did happen, and I'd have bet anything Michiko knew it.

"Another Collins-Peters rivalry. What do you want to bet the cafeteria will be making book on it?"

I gaped at her, and she bit her lip in exasperation. "Oh, come *on!* Isn't it about time you took off those blinders? Don't you know the rivalry between Brock and Zack has become the most fascinating item on the grapevine?"

"I don't believe it," I said slowly.

"Believe it. It's partly because Zack's such a hunk, and partly because a lot of kids are glad to see Brock get some competition for a change. They'll probably be neck and neck for this year's Citizenship Award. People have also been noticing how you've bloomed this year."

"Gorgeous and successful and famous, that's me," I said flippantly, to cover my embarrassment.

"Not to mention competed for." Michiko

giggled. "I know I shouldn't tell you this, but you know the way Joey's been wriggling himself into the thick of things whenever the crowd goes to your place? The wheeler-dealer's taking bets on who'll get to take you to the dance on New Year's Eve!"

I tore home, but I was so furious I didn't trust myself to tackle Joey. I cornered Mother instead, and she promised to have a long, stern talk with my little brother.

Michiko's comment about the rivalry jolted me, and I was jolted even more by a remark Scott Levine made when we were setting up for our next Theodore & Co. presentation. Our "political action committee," as Dad called us, was accepting bookings clear through to April, when the school board elections and the bond referendum would be held. "Any bets on whether Peters is going to be able to keep that good-natured-smile mask on till then?" Scott asked offhandedly.

"What do you mean?" I was startled, but not as startled as I'd have been before that talk with Michiko.

"Come on, Celia! It's like the football field all over again. The guy's not used to having rivals for the spotlight. It's probably bad enough sharing it with you, a girl," Scott said frankly, "but to be sharing it with a guy you date, who has as much on the ball as he does himself?"

I was getting sick and tired of hearing "Come on, Celia!"

Now that I'd been alerted, I couldn't help seeing what Scott and Michiko meant. Brock phoned me every night, and he was different on the telephone; more open, more unguarded. When I saw Zack alone, he was always spontaneous and funny. But on the platform, talking about the school bond issue, or at social affairs where all three of us were present, both of them changed. Brock became the polished politician, while Zack became what Mother, harking back to an old TV show, referred to as "young Dr. Kildare." Meaning scientific, dedicated, idealistic.

"Two male peacocks flaunting their plumage," Michiko said wisely. I told her that I was sick of the whole subject.

* * *

With the coming of December all this civic activity slowed down a little. We didn't have any choice—teachers piled on work before vacation. Even Mr. Oliver and Mr. Fontanazza got sticky about school assignments being done on time, so we couldn't sneak *Oakleaf* work into class anymore. Michiko was all wrapped up in her music—every orchestra she played in was having a holiday concert.

"We hardly ever get to talk now," I grumbled.

"This is just till the holidays. But I suppose after that you'll be busier than ever," Michiko said philosophically.

"I'll bet you're making time for David."

"He's a musician. He helps me with my practicing," Michiko replied demurely.

She didn't ask if I was making time for Brock and Zack, because she knew I was. It was turning into a regular square dance: Change partners and swing. The high school orchestra gave its concert—Zack took me, and Brock took Laurie. Brock took me to the '50s Sock Hop the *Oakleaf* sponsored. "I thought you'd be going with Laurie," I said involuntarily when he asked me.

"Laurie and I," Brock said, "aren't Siamese twins. As you ought to know by now. I could ask you, how come you aren't going with Zack the Hunk?"

Hunk, indeed. What kind of a monster had I created last summer, I thought, and giggled. Zack certainly wasn't a monster. "Oh, Zack's not wild about dancing," I said lightly.

"That," Brock replied, "I'm glad to hear."

When we arrived at the dance, Zack *was* there, with a spectacular blonde none of us had ever seen before. Hmmm, I thought, and wondered why I felt forlorn. I turned to Brock and batted my lashes at him, and Brock responded by pulling me close.

Laurie was at the hop with Pete Bayer, and if that bothered Brock it certainly didn't show. Walter Joyce, the sports editor, took business manager Jo Egan, and since neither of them had displayed any interest in the opposite sex before, this caused a minor flurry. We all went out for pizza afterward, but Brock soon suggested that we leave. We did *not* go straight home.

When we did get home, we parked in my driveway in our usual spot—just inside the entrance posts, with headlights off, far enough from the house so the dogs wouldn't bark and tell my family.

Brock ran his fingers through my hair. "So, what color flowers do you want for New Year's Eve?"

"What color—" I pulled myself up, my eyes snapping. "Brock Peters, if that's an invitation, couldn't you phrase it a little better?"

"It's what's known as 'winning by assumption,'" Brock said, grinning. "I'm going to write a book about it someday. We'll have to talk about that sometime, but not now. What about those flowers?"

"Now wait a minute. I haven't said I'm going with you. For all you know, I could already have a date."

"If you did, you'd have said so already." Brock knew me too well.

"And for all I knew, you could already have had a date with Laurie."

"Now *you* wait." Brock straightened, too. "Are you telling me I have to make a choice? I haven't told you to choose between me and Collins, have I? Because I know what you'd say." That was more than I knew, I thought confusedly. He pulled me close again. "Laurie's a great girl," he murmured against my hair. "But you have things she hasn't."

"Mmm . . . what?"

"Maybe I'll tell you sometime. Now, are you going to the dance with me or aren't you?"

We settled the question nonverbally.

Christmas was only a few days away. On Saturday we had our annual family expedition to buy a tree. This is one of the customs Mother clings to adamantly, and it sets us up in fine form for another Prendergast tradition: low-level squabbling that lasts up to the arrival of guests on Christmas Day. Mom's one of those people who think Christmas wouldn't be Christmas if the tree was trimmed earlier than Christmas Eve, and it drives us wild.

Around nine in the evening, the telephone rang. "I need rescuing," Zack said. "Mom called to ask if I minded if she accepted a dinner invitation. Of course I told her to go, but there's a minor problem. Our tree's not trimmed."

"Don't tell me you can't reach the top to put on the angel!"

"We have a star, not an angel, and that's not the problem. I have no sense of style, remember? This tree needs its image improved."

That was a lot of hooey, but it was a perfect excuse to escape from my own fireside. "If you'll come back here after, and help us, I'll be right there," I said, and hustled.

Compared to our house, Zack's was

serene. A fire burned on the hearth, there were Christmas carols on the stereo, and the start Zack had made on the tree looked fine. But it was so quiet, I could see why Zack hadn't wanted to trim the tree alone, and felt suddenly glad he and Aunt Lenore were coming to our house for Christmas dinner.

We hung the gold and silver and pale blue balls, arguing companionably and drinking hot spiced cider. By eleven-thirty the last garland was hung, and the mantel was decorated right down to the white-and-silver stockings. Zack cleared his throat.

"About the New Year's Eve dance . . ."

All of a sudden my throat choked up. I swallowed hard. "Oh, that's right, I meant to tell you!" I said with attempted airiness. "Brock crashed through with an invitation. So you won't have to force yourself to a dance for my sake." Something unreadable in his face made me add, nervously, "I appreciate the offer. But as you said a while ago, our deal worked out fine. Even Michiko says you're an established hunk. So you don't really need me anymore."

"That's not why you're not going with me," Zack said, not moving. "It's because Brock *does* need you—a lot more than you

172

need him. But maybe you need to have a guy need you to stroke his ego. Lord knows why."

I caught my breath, stunned. Then Zack's smile flashed.

"Did Michiko really say I was a hunk? Tell her thanks for the shot in the old morale. Anyway, I'm hoping Laurie Malone will go to the dance with me. That's what I was about to tell you. If you're going with Brock, maybe I'll have a chance!"

I reached home just as the grandfather clock was chiming midnight, and I did not have Zack with me.

Zack's words haunted me through the night and into Christmas morning. Fortunately, the morning provided plenty of distractions. There was the usual scramble to get the turkey in the oven and the chestnuts peeled. My grandparents arrived, and some cousins from Long Island. And in time for our five o'clock dinner, Aunt Lenore, and Zack.

Equivocal was a good word for the way I felt. Maybe *discombobulated* was even better.

In the evening a lot of our crowd went visiting back and forth. And the next morning, early, Michiko called to tell me she'd just heard through the grapevine that Zack was taking Laurie to the dance. "I know he was hoping to. I think it's great!" I said brightly.

Christmas week spun on its way. Before I knew it, it was New Year's Eve, and time for the dance.

I had a beautiful gown, far more beautiful than I could normally afford, thanks to Aunt Lenore's store discount. It was a sample dress of deep copper taffeta that made my eyes and hair glow like copper, too. I should have felt on top of the world, floating into the school gym on Brock's arm.

But I didn't. And I did not know why. As Zack had said a while back, everything had worked out, not just according to plan but according to my wildest dreams. Brock was even—if his words in the car that night could be believed—hinting about our going steady. The seniors had recently received their class rings. I might soon be wearing his. If I wanted to. Of course I wanted to, didn't I?

"I've been thinking," Brock whispered against my hair.

"About what?"

"Oh, a lot of things. I'll tell you some of them on our way home. Maybe." He gave that little chuckle that made my heart turn over. "But I guess I could tell you the non-personal ones now."

He swung me around, laughing. "I was talking to my dad last night. I've applied for admission to Rutgers, and a couple of New York City colleges, too, just to be safe. I'm going to live at home, and run for the Board of Education in April. Dad thinks I have a good chance. He won't let on, but he's proud as punch. And it's all thanks to you."

"I'm glad."

"You know what else I was thinking?" Brock went on. "That video documentary we put together to show around town really *is* good. Maybe your dad could get it shown on PBS, as a public affairs program, you know?"

I felt suddenly shy. "I don't know. I could ask."

"You do that," Brock said, and chuckled. He swung me around again, so my skirt fanned out in a swirl of copper. He was holding me so tight I could feel our two hearts pounding.

But as the orchestra segued into "Auld Lang Syne," and bells and whistles signaled the new year, I saw Zack and Laurie, together, over Brock's broad shoulder.

And I felt lonely.

FIFTEEN

The new year began, and it was different.

For one thing, teachers started piling on the work. Even Mr. Oliver was inconsiderate. Laurie and I started grumbling about how we wished we'd never thought of biweekly *Oakleaf*s. We saw a lot of each other, but two subjects we never touched on were Zack and Brock. I wasn't seeing as much of Zack because I was so busy; I wasn't seeing much of Michiko, either. Brock and the lobbying for the school bond issue filled the void, not to mention Brock's Board of Education campaign.

I talked to Dad about televising our documentary, and he was skeptical. "Public-access cable TV would be the best place for it. It's an amateur production. And it takes sides in a local political issue. That's a violation of journalistic neutrality."

"Dad! If it ran on public access, hardly anyone would see it. I'm not asking you to run it as an editorial, or as news." I took a deep breath. "It's a . . . a demonstration of civic responsibility by teenagers, and it's already attracted plenty of attention. And you said yourself the film was good!"

"I'll think about it," Dad said.

I told Brock. Brock was counting on it. That was one thing that troubled me about Brock: When a good idea came up, he took for granted that it would come true, just like that. Probably because things always did work that way for him. Or had, till this past football season.

Meanwhile, we plowed through school-work and exams, and plowed through snowdrifts. Booking three or four "political action committee" presentations at this time of year had not been a bright idea. Zack stopped coming to any, saying he was too busy, but Theodore continued as the star.

My mother made him a padded red slipcover, like a muff, to keep him warm.

"I wish I were as warm as he is," I grumbled one night, coming home through sleet. Brock took one hand off the steering wheel to pull me close. "That's a kind thought, but maybe not a wise one," I told him. "This road's like glass!"

Brock obediently pulled to the curb and parked, so he could warm me satisfactorily with both arms. "What's wrong with the little guy?" he asked presently, when I disengaged myself. We, if not the car, were getting overheated.

"Huh?" I asked blankly.

"Theodore. He looks like he's getting frostbite." He indicated a section of shell that was protruding from the turtle's snowsuit. I looked, then looked again.

"I think his shell's starting to crack. We'd better get him back to Zack, pronto. Brock, please hurry!"

He hurried more than was probably advisable, considering the weather. Zack looked at Theodore, now fast asleep, and frowned.

"Nobody's been squeezing him, have they?" I shook my head. "It could be the change of temperature. Maybe he'd better take a leave of absence for a week or so. You can keep your media circus spinning without him, can't you?"

"Of course," Brock said graciously. But he wasn't happy.

The sleet storms let up, and then we had the annual January thaw, complete with flooded cellars. "Why didn't anybody warn us about this?" Aunt Lenore groaned. Susie went swimming in the cellar and made herself an absolute mess, and Missy was afraid to wade through the lake that was our backyard. She sat on a pile of melting snow and screamed till I carried her back inside.

February came, and it turned cold again. The school bond issue heated up, and the first public hearing on the Dynachem expansion was held. It degenerated into a shouting match. The next day, along with news and feature coverage and lots of readers' letters, *The Record* ran a small editorial box saluting Oakdale High School students for their community spirit in working for an issue we believed in.

Two days later Dad greeted me at dinner with a grim smile. "I have an early Valentine's Day present for you. That film you kids put together is going on the air."

"Dad!"

"Don't thank me," Dad said. "It wasn't my idea, and I'm not sure it's a good one. The producer of our eight o'clock news show thought it up, and I was outvoted. It will run, with some cutting, as a public interest feature on Sunday night."

I flew to the telephone to spread the news. Brock was pleased, but not surprised. Laurie was thrilled, and Scott, thinking of college applications, was ecstatic. Zack wasn't home.

"He's gone down to Rutgers," Aunt Lenore told me. "Goodness knows what for! All I know is, he's obsessed by something. Probably some scientific experiment. He's been spending a lot of extra time at Dynachem, lately, you know. Can I give him a message?"

"Tell him our video is going to air on Dad's station Sunday." It was a letdown, not telling him the news myself, but it was only fair that Zack should alert the people at Dynachem himself tomorrow, before they heard it via the town grapevine.

School was buzzing the next day. Since Oakdale students were solely responsible for our public service film, the whole school basked in reflected glory. Even Mr. McPhail came to congratulate us at lunchtime. "Nice little shot in the arm for your own campaign, isn't it?" he asked Brock dryly.

"I can't deny that," Brock said frankly. "But that's not the most important thing." His eyes swept around the overcrowded cafeteria.

Mr. McPhail nodded. "Anything to help that bond issue go through! Nobody who isn't around here every day can possibly realize how much it's needed."

Zack agreed, but his face was somber. I wondered what was going on.

I caught up with him at his locker before he took off after school. "Zack, is something wrong?"

"No, of course not. Why?"

"I saw you at lunch. You looked worried. You still do."

"Maybe I'm just getting tired of keeping up the image."

"Don't give me that," I retorted half angrily. "I know you without the image, remember? What's the matter?"

To my surprise, he reached out and touched my hair lightly. "Don't worry. I just have something on my mind. A chemical problem."

"With Dynachem?"

"You could say that." It was all he'd tell me.

Whatever it was, I didn't get a chance to pump Zack any further. Then, the afternoon of the day our film was to be televised, he phoned.

"Are you alone? Can you come over?"

"Now?" We were going to be eating dinner in an hour.

"Now. It's important."

I hurried over, and Zack met me at the door. "I put the coffeepot on. And there's cake. Ma's out, but I'll do the honors."

"Never mind that. "What's up?"

"You'd better have some coffee first," Zack insisted, and he practically stood over me while I drank it. Then I put the cup down in the saucer firmly.

"Tell me. I can't stand this much more."

"You may have to," Zack said soberly. He went to his backpack and took out a sheaf of papers that he spread before me.

I looked at them blankly. "What are these?"

"Remember that weird spot on Theodore's

shell?" Zack asked. "It's spreading. And you know how that crack last summer wouldn't heal. I took him down to the School of Veterinary Medicine at Rutgers. He wasn't hit with a rock at all. It's a genetic problem. Caused by chemical pollutants."

I just stared at him.

"Pollution, Celia," Zack said gently. "In the water he was raised in—that his parents were raised in. I finally did what I meant to do last summer. I ran tests on the water in that stream."

"You mean...at *Dynachem?*"

Zack nodded. "There's been a malfunction in the chemical purification process somewhere. Maybe because of the layer of hardpan, a few feet down, that this whole area's built on. I never knew about that before the thaw, but it's the reason for all the flooding. Liquid can't seep away, so it stays here. And floods homes. And gets in reservoirs."

My mouth was dry. "Are you talking about PCBs?"

"Something like that. I won't try to explain the scientific terms. But I ran the tests, and a couple of professors at Rutgers are running more. If I'm right, all that stuff I was so sure of about Dynachem's model handling of chemical waste is wrong. If turtles have been affected, other wildlife may be, too. And in the long run, so might humans."

I didn't speak. My head was whirling.

"Celia," Zack said gently, "I'll have to report this to Dynachem tomorrow. I'll tell Bob Herskovitz first; he'll know where to take it from there. But I thought you'd want to tell your father."

"Why?"

"Because of the film," Zack said. "He may want to yank it. It gives a false picture of the Dynachem situation. And if the contamination's as bad as it well may be, there's no way Dynachem's marine products manufacturing plan can go ahead."

"No," I said dumbly. And then, louder, "*No*. Oakdale needs the expansion. The jobs, the money, everything—you know! The school bond issue...." My voice trailed off.

"You think I haven't thought about all those things?" Zack said. "You think I liked taking my findings down to Rutgers?"

"That's just it!" I was grasping at straws. "You can't be sure, not till your own tests are confirmed by experts. That's—scientific.

Please, please don't say anything till then! Because you could blow everything."

Not just the TV show tonight. The school bond issue. Zack's own future at Dynachem—he loved it there; he wanted a career there. Other people's jobs as well—suppose the Dynachem plant here had to shut down completely? Things like that had happened elsewhere, and I knew the whole town would be affected.

I wet my lips. "Zack, please. Just keep quiet till you have more evidence. That can't hurt anything. The expansion wouldn't get started for months and years yet, anyway. Talk to your boss. He'll know what to do. But don't just blow everything away in one fell swoop! There's too much at stake."

"It isn't honest to let the school bond issue be voted on with people thinking money's going to be coming in from Dynachem," Zack said uncomfortably.

He was right. "So we'll tell," I said reluctantly. "When we know for sure, we'll tell." I caught my breath. "Zack, I know you don't like him, but couldn't you let *Brock* break the news? He's running for the Board of Education on the school expansion issue, and he's the one who dreamed up the idea of kids campaigning. If *you* come out with this pollution story now, it won't just make him look like a fool, it will make some people wonder if he was lying all along."

It would also make people wonder whether Zack was cooking up a mess of sour grapes, but I didn't say that.

"He's not the only one who'll look like a fool," Zack said wryly. "I'm the one who babbled about how ecologically correct Dynachem was, remember?"

We just looked at each other, and the kitchen was so still the clock's ticking sounded like thunder.

"Okay," Zack said at last. "I'll keep my mouth shut tonight. I'll keep it shut till I get the results back from Rutgers, and I won't say anything then except to my boss. Not for Brock's sake. For Dynachem's. I owe them that."

And for my sake. The implication, unspoken, was behind Zack's words. "You'd better tell Peters about this *soon*," he added.

"I will," I said. "I promise." I stood up and buttoned the coat I'd never gotten around to taking off. Like an automaton, I walked to the door, then turned. "I almost forgot. Theodore."

"He'll be okay," Zack said. "The guys at Rutgers are making a plastic shell for him. Kind of a prosthesis."

I started to giggle, though it wasn't funny. Zack laughed, too. Then he came over, and turned my collar up around my neck and kissed me. And I walked home through the cold and dark.

I watched the film on PBS that evening, surrounded by family acclamation. And I felt like Judas.

SIXTEEN

After the television program finished, our phone started ringing. Aunt Lenore; Michiko; Brock. Not Zack. Whether that was because he was giving me time, as I'd begged him, or because he was angry that I hadn't told Dad to yank the show, I didn't know. It wasn't just our video, anyway. The newscaster narrator had gotten clips of CBS's interview with Brock and me, and he also added commentary lauding our public spirit. All that just made things worse.

Brock thought all of it was wonderful. That's because he didn't know. I tried to tell him, or at least I think I did. I tried to tell him all through the following week. Somehow, I didn't manage. Maybe I wasn't really trying.

I told myself it was because we were so busy. No one had time to talk, let alone listen. Brock's campaign for a seat on the Board of Education was gearing up, and it was attracting a lot of publicity. *The Record* even did a feature story on him.

Somewhere in the middle of all this came Valentine's Day. I got a big, beautiful, expensive valentine from Brock, and a little funny one from Zack and Theodore. I called Zack to say thank you and to ask how Theodore was doing.

"Theodore's fine, I think," Zack said. "He's back from Rutgers, wearing his new shell. He's thinking of collecting autographs on it. Have you talked to Brock?"

"Not yet. I will, I promise." I rushed on before Zack could protest. "Did you tell Mr. Herskovitz about your tests? What did he say?"

There was a momentary silence. "He said I did the right thing telling him," Zack said. "He said he'd report it to the vice presidents as soon as he had the data from the outside scientists."

"Do you have it yet?"

"Yes."

The way Zack said that, I didn't need to ask the results. "You're not going to talk about this to anyone else, are you?" I asked. Zack said no, not till Mr. Herskovitz said he could, but that I'd better warn Brock quickly before things got too hot.

A planning board open hearing on the Dynachem expansion was scheduled for the last week in February, then canceled because of a snowstorm. I breathed again. Brock spent two hours on the phone with me, furious at the weather for slowing up our campaigns. That's when I should have opened my big mouth and told him the bad news. But again I didn't.

Our campaigns. That was how I thought of them. The Dynachem expansion bid, the school budget, the school bond issue, and Brock's run for office were all merging into one in my mind. And I thought of them as *ours.*

The first Friday in March brought another informal dance. I was taking Brock. I came home from school late because of an *Oakleaf* staff meeting, and Mother met me in the hall with a strange expression on her face.

"I don't suppose you've seen tonight's *Record*, have you?"

I looked at her blankly. "Why?"

For answer she held out the county news section, opened to the second page. Across the bottom ran an update entitled "Oakdale Youths' Election Involvement" and, as a sidebar, an interview with Zack Collins, student scientist.

My heart lurched. My eyes raced along the lines of print.

"Nothing new, just an update," Mother said. "But if you ask me, Zack doesn't sound like Zack. He sounds as if he's trying *not* to say things."

She was exactly right.

"Nothing's gone sour at Dynachem, has it?" Mother asked, watching me closely.

"Oh, he's still wild about working there!" I said quickly, and escaped. I went to my room, closed the door firmly, and reached for the phone.

Zack knew why I was calling as soon as he heard my voice. "I didn't know the piece would come out like that. I was trying to be so careful not to do anybody any harm. But that reporter was determined to have something quotable about the Dynachem expansion. At least I didn't give her any-thing she could pin me down on."

That was the whole trouble. "Couldn't you have told her the same old spiel? At least until Mr. Herskovitz tells you to can it?" I asked despairingly.

There was a momentary pause. "No," Zack said at last. "No, I couldn't."

When Brock arrived to take me to the dance, he was furious. He'd seen the article and was in the frame of mind to think Zack was deliberately sabotaging him. "Stop it!" I said at last, sharply. Brock slowed the car to look at me in amazement.

"What's eating you?"

"We have to talk. Not here. Park some-where."

Brock complied without argument, then turned to me, his face taut. "What is it?"

After all my rehearsing, the brutal truth just burst out. "Dynachem's contaminating Oakdale with industrial waste. Something like PCBs, and it may be dangerous."

"*What?*"

"It's true," I said miserably. "Zack had tests done. Not just his own. By outside scientists."

"*Collins!*" Brock grabbed me. "How long have you known this?"

"Not long. Brock, you're hurting me!"

He released me quickly with a muttered apology. Then, his face stern, he took me through the whole story, step-by-step. When I was finished, his face was gray. "And you didn't tell me."

"I couldn't bear to. I didn't know how. Zack—"

Brock gave an angry laugh. "He must be gloating! He's looking forward to seeing me make a fool of myself."

"Brock, that's crazy! Zack feels awful. If it comes down to it, *he* looks like the fool. He's the one who started saying what a model citizen the Dynachem plant was."

"I'll bet he feels awful." Brock's mouth twisted. "He can't stand it that I took you away from him, can he? That he can't quite get ahead of me, no matter what he tries. So now he's trying this!"

"That's crazy!" I said again, shrilly. And then, getting myself under control, "Look, the important thing for all of us is not to freak out. Zack told his boss, but he's not talking otherwise; he's not allowed. Dynachem's doing an internal investigation and more testing. Maybe," I said with false optimism, "they'll be able to solve the whole problem before the planning board decision and the elections."

"I'm going to have my own tests done," Brock said grimly. "Definitely before the elections! We can't be sure the whole thing's not a dirty trick!" He released the brake and gunned the car into high gear.

The gym looked as it did for most school dances: dim, colored lights; a strobe; crepe paper; a semipro deejay. The noise and the flickering lights were, blessedly, like insulation against thinking. So were Brock's arms. I was very glad that much of the evening was spent in slow dancing. I was vaguely aware of Michiko dancing with David Perlman, and of Walter Joyce solemnly box-stepping with Jo Egan. Other than that, I tried to blot out consciousness of anything except the music and Brock's arms. Then I stumbled, and we bumped into something, and I felt Brock go stiff.

Not something. Someones. Plural. Zack and Laurie. Why was I surprised?

"Watch what you're doing!" Brock muttered savagely.

"I try to," Zack answered stiffly. And all of a sudden Brock's veneer of calm was gone.

"Oh, sure you do! The way you did in that

interview? Celia told me what dirty tricks you've been up to, and I'm warning you—"

"It's not a trick," Zack snapped. "This is dead serious!"

"You bet it is!" Brock grabbed Zack's arm. "Too serious to let some punk louse it up just because he can't stand the competition! Just remember, buddy, you're not fooling around with an amateur. So if you're going to fight dirty—"

Zack pushed away Brock's arm. At least that's what I think he meant to do. Only Brock moved, and the push landed against his chest. Brock swung at Zack.

All of a sudden the dance looked like the aftermath of a soccer match.

Somebody screamed. Somebody shoved me. And then Michiko and David and Scott Levine were pulling Brock and Zack apart. Laurie grabbed Brock, pinning his arms down, talking hard and fast, as I stood frozen.

David got Zack off the floor just as Mr. McPhail bore down on us. "What's going on?" the principal demanded.

"It's a personal matter," Zack answered stiffly.

"Peters?"

"Like he said. It's personal." Brock's jaw was set.

"My office. First thing Monday morning," Mr. McPhail snapped. "As for right now—"

I started to shake. Then Michiko's hand was on the middle of my back. "Girls' locker room. Fast!" she hissed, and steered me out.

Once in the green-and-gray bleakness of the locker room, Michiko stood aside tactfully while I shook and sniffled. "I don't suppose there's any use asking what it's all about?" she inquired at last. I shook my head.

The door opened, and Laurie came in. "McPhail's thrown the boys out," she said in a subdued tone. "I'm leaving, too. Celia? Brock's waiting to see what you want to do."

I didn't answer. "Tell him to go," Michiko said. "David and I will see that she gets home." Laurie nodded and walked out, and Michiko sat and waited while I splashed water on my face and pulled myself together. Then she went and got David and we left.

When I reached home, my parents took one look and read me like a book. *"Yes?"* Mother commented in that way she has. Her eyes were gentle.

"Brock and Zack got in a fight. Don't ask me to explain. Not yet." I bolted.

196

When I was a little kid, I sometimes used to get a convenient cold or headache when there was something to avoid. I'm ashamed to say I did that Saturday. Rain slashed at the windows, echoing my mood, as I huddled underneath the covers and tried hard not to think. The phone rang several times that morning. At eleven, my mother appeared.

"Brock wants to know if you're all right. So does Zack. He's called three times, and he wants to see you."

"I don't want to see him," I muttered.

"You'll have to," Mother said. "He's downstairs now."

So I pulled on an old bathrobe and plodded down, regardless of uncombed hair and red eyes. It was, after all, only Zack.

He was standing in the living room. Mother, blessedly, removed Joey and herself. Even more fortunately, Dad wasn't home. Zack and I stood, several feet apart, looking at each other.

"Celia, I'm sorry," Zack said at last.

I heard my voice say icily, "You should be. You weren't going to spill the beans till your boss told you to. You were going to give me a chance to figure out a way to salvage Brock's election and the school bond issue.

197

And then you shot your mouth off to the newspaper."

"I didn't shoot my mouth off!" Zack snapped. "I very carefully avoided the whole pollution issue! Can I help it if that reporter read between the lines? I'm very sorry, but I'm not as good at wearing a phony mask as you are."

"Zack!"

"And you know what? I don't want to be. Did you hear yourself just now? Brock's election. Even the school bond issue. Do you really think those are the most important things at stake here?"

All I could say was, "Get out. Just get out."

He did.

SEVENTEEN

———◆———

Brock and Zack got two-day suspensions for fighting at the school dance. I got a headache and a very confused conscience.

Brock was furious about the suspension. It was not going to look good on his record, and it meant he had to take an *F* on a test he missed. I suspected that secretly he was relieved to have those two days free, because his election campaign went into overdrive. He had kids distributing posters, writing press releases, and handing out fliers. On the Monday of his suspension, I went over to his house after an *Oakleaf* session and found him missing while the rest of his minions slaved. On Tuesday, when we arrived from school, he had a whole new angle to promote, and a lot of good statistics on the benefits of enlarging the school and implementing Mr. McPhail's pet programs.

Aunt Lenore had mixed feelings about Zack's being temporarily kicked out. She didn't think it would look great on his record, either, and she was worried because Zack wouldn't tell her why he'd punched Brock and why he was looking like a thundercloud.

"Other than that," Mother said ruefully, "I think she's secretly relieved that her weird little kid's turned out to be so normal!" She frowned severely at my little brother and his friends, who were racing the circuit of our ground-floor rooms and yelling. "Lenore doesn't know when she's lucky!"

I knew about Zack from Mother, not from him, because Zack and I weren't speaking. Maybe I should say, we weren't noticing each other's existence when we passed in the halls. The whole school knew, of course, particularly since he was sitting with Laurie Malone's crowd at lunch, and not with mine. Even Dorothy Sheridan, whose curiosity is limitless, knew better than to ask me questions.

At least nobody was feeling sorry for me.

Brock made it very clear we were a couple, not a passing phase. I wished I understood a little better how I felt.

On the Saturday after the fateful dance, Brock telephoned. "Can you come over? I have to talk to you."

"We're going out tonight, aren't we? Can't—"

"This won't keep, and it's private. Please come."

Brock met me at the door and led me to the small room his father used as a home office. Right now it was overflowing with materials for Brock's campaign. But he turned instead to a locked drawer in the desk and took out a folder containing Xeroxes. "I took my own samples of the water in that Dynachem stream," Brock said. "And soil samples, and a bunch of other things. Somebody my dad knows owns an independent testing outfit, and I asked him to do an analysis. I didn't tell him where the samples came from or why I wanted them. I didn't even tell my father. But I think you'd better read the results."

I'm taking chemistry, and it isn't rubbing off on me too well. But I recognized the lab report format. I could recognize a number of the formulas and the abbreviations. And there were some things nobody could mistake. Such as: *Level of contamination in water, 0.03.* Such as: *We find no evidence of any chemicals in the samples other than the amounts normal to the geographical area. Conclusion: No danger predicted to humans or animals.*

I looked up from the folder, frowning. "Brock, why?"

"Why, what?" Brock asked. "Why did I have the tests done? Because I didn't trust your friend Collins. He's been trying to force a showdown between us ever since he came to Oakdale. Why do you think he told you a lie about the contamination?"

"Zack wouldn't lie," I said stubbornly.

Brock made an impatient gesture. "Wake up, Celia! Anybody will do anything if the stakes are high enough!" Then he saw my face, and continued in a softer tone, "Maybe it wasn't a lie. Maybe he loused up his tests somehow, or got his samples contaminated, because he'd lost his scientific detachment."

I didn't speak, and after a moment he went on. "Look, Celia, I don't want to hurt the guy if I don't need to. I don't want you hurt. I'll keep quiet about those tests of his so long as he does. But I can't let the school bond issue, and all the other benefits Oakdale can get from a Dynachem expansion, go down the drain because of a mistake, can I?"

"No, you can't," I said dully.

We didn't talk about any of this when we were out that night. Actually, we didn't do much talking about anything.

On Sunday afternoon, after a stiff battle with myself, I dialed the Collinses number.

Aunt Lenore answered. "He's out. I don't know where or for how long. Can I give him a message, Celia?"

"Tell him—tell him I've seen another set of test results. They show his answers are all wrong." Let Aunt Lenore think I was talking about school tests.

Hours later, the phone woke me. "What do you mean, my results are wrong?" Zack demanded.

"What I said. Brock had tests done, too. They show no higher contamination levels in soil or water than would be normal."

"That's weird." Zack's voice wasn't angry anymore. He was back to being a scientist, intent and puzzled. "Where did he have the tests done? Did you get copies?"

"At a lab he heard of through his dad. No, I didn't. Brock says he won't make them public unless he has to, and he's keeping them locked up so they can't leak out. He really doesn't want to resort to dirty politics."

"Right," Zack said with more than a touch of sarcasm.

"Zack? What's happening about all this at Dynachem?"

"I don't know," Zack said flatly. "Bob Herskovitz talked to the division vice president and was told to sit tight. I know Dynachem's doing lots of tests. I've seen geologists out taking samples." He paused. "The results probably won't come through till after the planning board votes on the expansion."

The next week was packed with political activity. There was a public hearing about the school budget, which threatened to become a riot. Conflicting views about the nature and purpose of a good education were hurled back and forth. The next night the planning board met, and spectators overflowed the meeting room. The Dynachem expansion was the third item on the agenda, but when eleven o'clock came, the board was still arguing over whether to allow another fast-food place in town. A special meeting on the Dynachem issue was hastily scheduled for the following Monday night.

To cap all this off, I'd promised the Civics

Club that I'd pass out fliers promoting the school budget at the supermarket two nights that week. And I had a major chemistry exam on Tuesday. I was beginning to detest chemistry more than ever.

By Monday afternoon I was ready to jump out of my skin. So when Michiko begged me to go with her to a music audition down at Montclair College, I leaped at the chance.

I couldn't attend the audition itself; she just wanted me to hold her hand in transit. So when Michiko and her violin disappeared into the music building, I took myself across to Sprague Library and tried to study for my chem exam. The symbols swam before my eyes. Too many of them had unpleasant associations.

On an impulse I went to the computer and looked up books on chemical pollution. I don't know why; maybe I just wanted to understand the issues better. Whatever the reason, I took a heavy armload over to the nearest carrel and started plowing through.

I was leafing through the seventh volume when something penetrated through my fog. I stared. And froze. And stared again.

As I said, I'm no hotshot at chemistry, but I can recognize when the format of three consecutive pages looks alarmingly familiar. When the same symbols recur in the precise same patterns. *Images.* That's what those pages were, and for good or ill I'd become an expert, hadn't I, on images and design?

I could certainly recognize when a section of a report on tests for chemical pollution of soil and water samples ended with the exact same sentences that were seared across my memory.

We find no evidence of any chemicals in the samples other than the amounts normal to the geographical area. Conclusion: No danger predicted to humans or animals.

It was the same report that Brock had told me was an independent lab's report on the samples he had taken at Dynachem. I couldn't prove it, not yet, but I knew it.

I might need to prove it.

Like an automaton, I took the book to the Xerox machine and made copies. Like an automaton, I returned the book, and all the others, to the reference desk.

I was cramming for my chemistry exam when Michiko came to claim me. I rode home in silence. Michiko didn't notice; now ∪nat the audition was over, she was a chatterbox. I went into the house and straight up the stairs despite Mother's reminder that it was already six-fifteen and the Dynachem meeting began at seven.

I went directly to the telephone and dialed Zack's number.

"Oh, I'm sorry, Celia. He's gone out, and he won't be back all evening." Aunt Lenore's voice was solemn. "That Herskovitz man from Dynachem that Zack likes so much had a stroke at work this afternoon. He's been taken to some hospital in New York. Zack was so relieved the meeting tonight was called off, so he could go in to the hospital himself, right from work."

"The meeting's called off?" I repeated blankly.

"Yes, someone telephoned shortly before five to say so. I called Zack at Dynachem to let him know." Her voice quickened. "Didn't anyone notify you, Celia?"

"No, they didn't," I said slowly. I went downstairs and told my parents. Mother looked puzzled; Dad, skeptical. He went to the phone and called somebody he knew on the planning board.

"The meeting's on as scheduled," he said, returning.

"Then why . . . ?" Mother frowned.

"Sounds as if someone wanted to make sure Zack wasn't there," Dad said, looking straight at me.

"Excuse me," I blurted to my mother, and I ran out. Not far; just to Aunt Lenore's. When she heard what I wanted, she brought it to me. I returned home and ate a fast dinner. And then I went to the meeting, and Dad went with me.

The meeting was jammed. The lawyers for Dynachem pleaded their case, and a lawyer for a group calling itself Citizens for the Preservation of Oakdale said his piece. And people talked, and argued, and shouted, and asked questions.

Somebody squeezed onto the bench beside me. Brock. He looked jubilant and ready for a challenge. It was the way he looked last year at the start of each football game. "I was afraid you weren't going to show up," he whispered. "I just spotted you. I need you here for luck!"

"Do you?" I whispered back. And then, "What about Zack? Did you need him not here?"

Brock looked disconcerted. Then he chuckled. "Pretty smart, wasn't I? Anything's fair when it comes to fighting for what really matters."

"Is it?" I asked. Brock's eyes fell on my lap.

"What's in that box? Your dinner?" He laughed again, and whispered, "I'll take you out for a real meal afterward, to celebrate."

I didn't answer.

The night went on. The noise went on. Brock's hand went up, and then he rose. The presiding chairman looked at him with something like relief. "In closing we'll hear from a young man who's demonstrated a great deal of concern for Oakdale's welfare," he said firmly. "Mr. Peters?"

Brock stepped forward easily, adjusting his tie. "Thank you, Mr. Chairman. I appreciate the chance to speak for Oakdale's future." He went on from there, painting a glowing picture of a growing, thriving city with a growing, internationally successful chemical company to pay the bills. Only the picture didn't glow so much for me right now.

Then it came, what I'd dreaded yet expected. An interruption from the audience with a question about industrial pollution and public safety.

"The attorneys from Dynachem have already explained that there is no reason for concern," Brock said. A ground swell of murmuring interrupted him. Then Brock's smile flashed. "Actually," he confessed disarmingly, "I was starting to get worried, too. I mean, you hear rumors, and I've been going around 'building my political future' on what we'd been told." He gave the words we'd all heard muttered about him the twist of an inside joke. "So I took it on myself to check things out."

He started telling, in almost the same exact words he'd used with me, about the "independent analysis" he'd paid to have done, and the clean-bill-of-health results.

It wasn't me who interrupted. Not consciously. Something inside of me brought me to my feet, some other Celia whom I hadn't known, or had maybe lost, who was saying in a clear, carrying tone, "That isn't true."

Several hundred heads swiveled toward me. "The test results Brock's talking about are fakes," I said. "There is pollution at Dynachem. Maybe their lawyers here haven't been told yet, but the company knows it. They're checking into it. I'm sorry to have to say it, but it is true. And I'm sorry to tell you there's already been one casualty."

I opened the box I'd brought and held aloft Theodore, with his shiny new plastic, made-at-Cook-College-School-of-Veterinary-Medicine shell.

EIGHTEEN

———◆———

That did it. Everyone knew about Theodore, local celebrity and symbol of Dynachem's model environmental record. Everyone knew about Celia Prendergast, activist for teen involvement and the Oakdale school system and Dynachem expansion. All thought of adjourning the meeting was swept away.

All these weeks, while Brock had been stonewalling, I'd been like someone frantically plugging a leak in the dike. Now I'd pulled the plug, and the flood burst through. Within fifteen minutes, the chairman of the planning commission had turned me inside out. The only reason the Dynachem lawyers and members of the audience didn't get to cross-examine me was because the chairman wouldn't let them.

By the time he was finished, there wasn't one thing I knew about this whole mess that everyone in the room didn't also know. Except I did manage to keep from telling why I was so sure Brock's facts were inaccurate. I just kept saying Zack's report gave different results, so Brock's had to be wrong. Finally, the lawyer for the town whispered to the chairman, and the chairman gaveled the hearing to a close.

Dad took my elbow and started steering me through the crowd as reporters began plowing toward us. Brock was separated from me by a wall of people, for which I was profoundly grateful. All I wanted to do was get back home.

Out in the hall Dad steered me toward an unmarked door. It led through a custodian's storeroom to a flight of service stairs, and then into the town police station. We exited from there into the parking lot. "This way," Dad said, turning me toward our car.

Before we reached it, a voice called sharply, "Not so fast!"

Brock actually vaulted through one of the hall's ground floor open windows. He cleared the space between us with varsity speed, and grabbed my arm. Dad didn't stop him. That's one thing I'll always remember: Dad had enough confidence in me to let me handle this without his interference.

"Do you realize what you've done?" Brock demanded. "You've shot down the bond issue and the school and me in one fell swoop. Over nothing! *Why?* What are you trying to do to me, anyway?"

All of a sudden everything fell into place. "Not *to you*," I said distinctly. "*For Oakdale*. And not over nothing. If you want to know why, check *Environmental Planning for the Next Millennium* by G.B. Hodges, pages two hundred seventeen to two hundred nineteen. Or go home and take a look at them in your locked desk drawer!"

"Is *that* what this is all about?" He actually looked flabbergasted. "So I fudged a little. I had to, didn't I, to keep you in line?"

I couldn't speak. But something in my expression made his face change. It was so weird. I felt as if I were watching one of those science-fiction movies in which familiar features dissolve like gel or putty to reveal the alien beneath.

Even Brock's voice changed. It suddenly was vicious. "For *Oakdale!* Don't give me that garbage! You've been feeding me that line all year, you and your opportunistic pal! I don't know what you're really after, but it sure isn't this town's welfare. That was just an act." His breath whistled as he drew it in. "I have to hand it to you, lady. I thought I knew you, but you sure took me in!"

"I wasn't putting on any act," I said quietly. "Neither was Zack. He couldn't." Even as I said it, I realized that was true. Oh, I'd changed our images last summer, but that was all I had changed—outer images. Zack was, and always would be, the same old Herbert Zachary Collins, regardless of packaging. And me? The repackaging Aunt Lenore had taught me had been like the fancy costumes I put on for Halloween when I was little: They'd released me from my own self-image to let me be who I really was.

And Brock? I'd been taken in by his packaging, too. Beneath the pride, beneath the tenderness in his eyes, beneath the smile, was—what? "I don't know you, either," I said slowly. "I don't think you even know yourself. The bond issue, and all those jobs Dynachem would bring, don't really matter to you, any more than contamination matters. All you really care about is winning. And yourself."

And I turned, and got in the car, and we drove away, with Brock's parting "You're nothing but a phony!" ringing in my ears.

End of story, as far as Brock and I were concerned.

* * *

Life didn't end. Life went on. I didn't dare stay home from school the next day because of that chemistry test. The halls were buzzing, but I avoided having to talk to people. Brock cut school.

The planning board met in closed session the following day and deferred any decision on Dynachem's expansion until they had detailed studies on the proposal's environmental impact. The studies would be made by an independent research firm hired by Oakdale and paid by Dynachem. "That," Dad said when he read this in the newspaper, "will stall things for years."

School elections arrived. The bond issue was voted down. The school budget squeaked through, barely. Brock was defeated in his bid for a seat on the school board. Apparently, even without spilling the truth about the falsified report, I'd destroyed his credibility.

"It's a sad thing," Dad said. For a crazy minute I thought he meant he was sorry Brock had lost. Then he added, "That kid's lack of ethics has ruined any other teen's chances of being elected to anything in this town for a long time."

I thought Brock's dirty trick was going to escape detection. But I'd overlooked the power of the *Oakleaf*, which I'd been partly responsible for unleashing. Pete Bayer, on his own, decided to find out what had made me blow the whistle. Piece by piece, he tracked down what I'd been doing those past few days. He tracked me to the college library, where you have to sign for reference books you look at. He found the books I'd gone through; he found out Brock had looked at the same ones earlier. He found pages 217 to 219, and put two and two together. And wrote an article.

Of course, he couldn't prove that was the report Brock had shown me, so he didn't accuse Brock of that. He just raised questions. The story ran on the front page of the *Oakleaf*, and I didn't know about it till the issues were distributed in the cafeteria. I was glad of that. I also felt like a fool.

"That's the end of Brock's getting the Citizenship Award," Michiko commented, not looking in my direction. Somebody said it wasn't fair, and somebody else snorted. People began pointing out past instances of Brock's self-interest. The king had been dethroned.

As for me, I felt as if I were walking around school naked, all the images I'd been hiding behind blown away: Celia, the confident activist; Celia, plain vanilla. Nobody likes the person who points out the idol has feet of clay.

To my astonishment, a circle of support formed around me. Michiko stood by me, even though I'd completely forgotten to go to one of her most important concerts. Beth and Dorothy were still there. Michiko's David sort of adopted me as a sister. The *Oakleaf* staff—even Laurie, who had good reason to resent me—stood by me. People I'd worked with on various things this year started calling me just to talk, coming over, hanging around. Scott Levine asked me out. I went, and it was fun.

The one person who wasn't around was Zack. Oh, I saw him, of course, because we were in school together and our families were so close. But when we talked, it was just surface chitchat. We never were alone.

I did know that Zack's principal reaction to my whistle-blowing was relief. The contamination he'd found on the Dynachem grounds was now public knowledge, as he'd thought it should be, without his having to break his pledge to Bob Herskovitz. I had taken that burden off his shoulders, and off Mr. Herskovitz's shoulders, too, though a bit late. He had been smack in the middle of situation ethics, too, and maybe that contributed to his stroke. He was recovering, but slowly, and whether he'd be able to work again was uncertain.

I knew all that from Mother and Aunt Lenore, but I'd have known Zack's relief just from looking at him. What I didn't know was how he felt about me. I wanted to tell him how sorry I was, and what a fool I'd been to value Brock more than him. But I didn't. Maybe it was pride. Or shame. Or embarrassment. Maybe I was just plain chicken.

When I looked at Zack, I was careful not to let our eyes meet. And he was usually with Laurie Malone.

I went out with Scott Levine again.

Brock was being consoled by a curvy freshman. The senior prom came along in the middle of May. Brock had asked me to it back in February, but he didn't mention it now and I didn't either. I went to it with Pete Bayer. Brock took the freshman, and they spent the evening publicly making out. Zack took Laurie.

Cut to June. Graduation was the second Wednesday, and the awards assembly was held that morning. Brock got his football letter even though he'd been sidelined by injury halfway through the season. That was all he got. The coveted Citizenship Awards, with accompanying scholarships, went to Laura Teresa Malone and Herbert Zachary Collins.

Graduation was at seven, on the football field. I wore the off-white T-shirt dress I'd bought last summer, and I went to the ceremony alone. Michiko was playing in the orchestra, and I didn't want anyone with me, anyway.

Afterward, as always, there was a jam of people and of traffic. Kids were trying to sneak looks into the gym, where the Graduation Ball was to be held. It was always planned and provided by the parents, and the theme was always top secret. I didn't try to look. I tried to get away without anybody stopping me, and in the process I practically ran down Laurie Malone.

She was still in her gown, dangling her cap by its tassel and carrying a bouquet of roses, and she looked very pretty. I said, "Congratulations for the Citizenship Award," and she hugged me.

"I wouldn't have had a chance of getting it if it hadn't been for all you've helped me do this year! With five kids in our family, the scholarship's a godsend. I know it is for Zack, too."

"Yes, I know." My voice was getting thick. "Have fun at the ball, you two," I said, as brightly as I could manage, and started off.

Laurie stopped me. She said, "Celia," firmly, took hold of me, and pulled me to one side. "I'm not going to the ball with Zack," she said. "I invited Keith Rawsen. We go out a lot when he's home from college. Zack didn't want to go with me, anyway."

While I was figuring out what to say, she said in a rush, "Look, I'll probably get killed for telling you, but I know about that bargain you made with Zack. How you agreed to make him look popular to keep his mother off his case," she added, and I breathed again. At least he hadn't told her about plain vanilla. "Zack thinks you did it only because you're so kind and noble. Men can be awfully dense! But so can some women!" Laurie looked me squarely in the eyes. "Zack isn't going to the ball. He doesn't want to go unless it's with the girl he really cares about. And if you don't know who that is, you're really dumb!"

I went home, sat down in the wicker rocker on the porch, and wrestled with my pride. *Dumb.* I really was, wasn't I, where some things were concerned. After all that had happened, I was still worrying about my image.

The sun sank, the sky turned gray and lilac, and the air grew cooler. And at last I got up and walked down the driveway, along the street (carefully avoiding the Peterses' place) to the Collinses' house. No one was home.

My feet seemed to have gone on automatic pilot, and what they did was retrace the route I'd taken all those months ago, last July, past the rhododendron bushes into Dynachem's private drive. He was where I'd known he would be, down by the water's edge communing with the geese. But then, we always had been on the same wavelength, deep down, hadn't we?

221

"You wouldn't have a plastic bag with you, would you?" I called before I lost my nerve.

Zack turned. He was wearing the correct crew shirt, the correct jeans, but he was still Zack, and all at once I wasn't nervous anymore.

"What's the bag for?" Zack asked cautiously.

"For Theodore. He deserves to go to the ball, don't you think, after all he's been through. And he can't go stark naked. Think of his image!" I was talking very fast, for I was breathless. "Of course there's one catch. You and I will have to go along to chaperone him."

Zack just stood there. "I thought you didn't want to see me anymore. You told me to get out of your life, remember?"

"Laurie's right. You *are* dense. I never said anything about getting out *forever.*" I took a deep breath. "I thought scientists always double-checked everything, just in case a mistake was made." He started coming toward me, hesitantly, and I added, "That's what I should have done. Not been taken in by a glittering image, just like you warned me. But at least give me credit for knowing the difference between real gold and a paint job, once the mists have cleared. The real gold's what I discovered right here, and it's what I want. If you do."

Zack took three more steps toward me. "About the ball. I didn't rent a tux."

"That doesn't matter. Wear anything you like."

His eyes took on a sly look. "Anything?"

"Anything!" I threw caution to the winds.

"Okay," Zack said amiably. "Let's go home and dress. Pick you up in half an hour. You can wear that orangey thing you had on at the New Year's Eve dance. It looked real nice."

So he'd noticed that. I took a fast shower and donned the copper taffeta, my heart singing. The doorbell rang as I was applying the prescribed "taupey smudges around the eyes." Mother, in a very enigmatic voice, called up, "Darling, your escort's here."

I started downstairs. And stopped. Zack was wearing a turn-of-the-century black tailcoat, top hat, and opera cloak, all of which I recognized from the Christmas window display at Aunt Lenore's store. His proper white bow tie was set dashingly beneath the collar of his beloved jumpsuit, spanking clean. An elegant silver-topped cane set off the splendor of heavy orange crepe-soled shoes.

"They match your dress," Zack said complacently, as I stared. In one hand he held a bouquet of orange and white flowers from Aunt Lenore's back garden. In his other arm was Theodore, rakishly wrapped in an orange ribbon with a shiny bow. A white daisy was stuck through the bow.

"His boutonniere. You said to bring him," Zack said firmly. His eyes were wicked.

I looked and I looked, and all of a sudden laughter bubbled from deep inside, like a dam bursting. "Come on, we're late already! People will think we're crazy, but what else is new?"

Theodore had a great time at the Graduation Ball. Everybody kept borrowing him, which was just as well. Zack and I weren't in the mood for chaperoning. As a matter of fact, we probably added several interesting facets to our images that night. So what? *We* knew who we were. What was more important, we knew what we had between us was no business arrangement. Far from it!

Even so, we parked at the lookout for quite a while on our way home. As Zack says, it never hurts to check and recheck the evidence, where chemistry's concerned!